THE PORTALS
OF PARADISE

THE PORTALS OF PARADISE

BRIAN STABLEFORD

WILDSIDE PRESS

Published by Wildside Press LLC.
www.wildsidebooks.com

I

THE MUTE DARK LADY

My uncle and I reached Venice, where I was to meet the Devil for the first and perhaps the only time in my life, later than we had originally planned, our itinerary having fallen behind schedule while passing through the Austrian Tyrol before we descended into Lombardy. There we had made haste, cutting out Verona entirely, but we only arrived in the city on the Friday of the Carnival, with only four days to Shrove Tuesday and the end of the celebration.

We had no way of knowing at the time, of course, that only ten years thereafter the Carnival would be abolished, during the brief period of Austrian rule that preceded Napoleon's conquest, and would only be resurrected after a long interval, as a meager shadow of its former self. We had no idea, in fact, that the whole of Europe was about to suffer a long political upheaval, and that Paris, where we had stayed for three months—which was by no means untypical for those undertaking the Grand Tour in those distant days—would be overtaken by Revolution in 1789, less than a year after our safe return to England.

We were, however very keenly aware throughout our Tour that the world was in a process of dramatic and drastic change, and that the legacy of the Renaissance, the supposed objective of study facilitated by the Tour, was already afflicted by Senescence—or, as the newly fashionable terminology had it, by Decadence. We had viewed Paris very much in that frame of mind, and we arrived in Venice with that consciousness in the forefront of our thoughts.

I can say "we," because my uncle Jerome was as fully conscious of the rapidity of social change as I was; how he could it be otherwise, given that he was the youngest partner in the firm of Bowlands and Sons of Bristol. In that capacity, he had been an active participant in the spectacular enrichment that had converted a moderately prosperous family firm—which hardly warranted the term of "Merchant Adventurers" that my grandfather loved to apply to himself—into a seriously wealthy concern, as demand for American cotton had increased so rapidly in consequence of new spinning and weaving machinery and novel means of powering that machinery. Nevertheless, his awareness of that change and his attitude to it differed considerably from mine.

"My dear Gabriel," he had said to me more than once since he left Paris, "what you call Decadence has been with us for a century and more, and has always been an essential aspect of the mythology of the Grand Tour. When your father and I made the Tour after graduating from Oxford, twenty-some years ago, France had just been defeated in the Seven Years War, and had lost many of her possessions in the Americas and much of her influence in Africa and India. The Court of Versailles was said to be a moral cesspit and the nation was thought then to be in the final throes of its Decadence. Venice was in the grip of a slower but similarly irrevocable decline, and was also said, exactly as it is now, to represent the epitome of Italianate Decadence, the perfect image of the final phase of the gaudy corruption of European civilization. But *plus ça change, plus c'est la même chose*, as they say in your beloved France. The collapse is always impending, but never actually comes."

I am not reporting that now in order to try and make Uncle Jerome seem foolish, or even short-sighted, because I certainly did not have the slightest inkling of the imminence of the Revolution and the subsequent advent of Napoléon Bonaparte myself, but merely to illustrate a difference of attitude between the two of us, consequent on our belonging to different generations.

"The point, Uncle," I replied to his sermons, "is not simply that an old order is decaying, but that within the decay, new and different life is springing forth. Even individuals, if you believe the mysticism of the Church, do not truly die, but are merely transfigured, bodily death merely conducting their souls to paradise or Hell, but that is far more true of cultures and civilizations, which very rarely suffer abrupt termination, but are always subject to strange metamorphoses."

I really did talk like that in those days, even at the age of twenty-one. You might think that I am a pompous old fool now, and that I am fully entitled to be one as I approach my dotage, but I have always been prone to such rhapsodies. My uncle, as I have just illustrated, was not immune to the tendency himself—he too had inevitably fallen under the pontificating influence of his father, Archibald Bowlands, although he had not exaggerated it in his turn, as he often accused his brother George, my father, of having done. With an ancestry and a home environment like that, what chance did I have?

To the impulsion of that heredity, though, must be added certain idiosyncrasies of my own, which came from I know not where, and of which my grandfather, father and uncle all disapproved.

Nowadays, of course, I have a label that I can apply to my youthful eccentricities: I was a Romantic. In those days, however, the term had not been refined in the sense it acquired when it was applied collectively to Byron, Scott, Shelley, Coleridge and their ilk. If I had laid claim to any self-description, it would have been the French title of *philosophe*, which did not have the same range of application as the English "philosopher" but was more elastic, with all sorts of radical connotations.

At twenty-one, I was ambitious to be a playwright—and you can probably imagine what effect that had on my elders, who saw me as the destined inheritor of a petty commercial empire—but not in the sense that an Englishman of today would view a playmaker for the London theater as a mere craftsman. In those days, all the great French *philosophes*, including the not-long-dead Monsieur de Voltaire and the still very-much-alive Monsieur Mercier, were dramatists, who regarded the theater as the most important form of cultural expression, and the cradle of new ways of thinking and feeling.

The *philosophes*—especially such pioneers as Jean-Jacques Rousseau and Monsieur Diderot—were well aware of the Decadence of the theatrical tradition within which their contemporaries were working, of the stifling restriction of the categorization of tragedy and comedy and the conventions of imitation that borrowed so heavily from Classical models and sources. They were also well aware, however, of the scope that there was for innovation within the interstices of those very conventions, especially for the development of the new theatrical genre of drama championed by Monsieur Diderot, and for the moral reappraisal of the stock figures of tragedy and comedy in the light of newer ways of thinking.

But I'm boring you, aren't I? I'm being pedantic, as usual. What you want to hear about is how I met the Devil during the Carnival of Venice, and how I became embroiled in the adventure of the Portals of Paradise. You want to know about the legacy of the *bravi* and the strange aspirations of the men with no eyes, and the *femme fatale* who beguiled me into playing a part in their bizarre quest because she mistook me for an angel. If you're to understand all that, however, you do need to know a little about me, about the various ideas I had at the time, and the nature of my fascination with the theater. In the interests of not losing my audience before I've even begun to tell the story, however, I'll postpone as much of that background information as I can, and leak it into the story by degrees as I go along. I shall not be able to suppress my pontificating tendencies entirely, I fear, but as I'm an old man now, falling apart myself, I feel entitled to ramble a little, on occasion.

I can't begin the story with my encounter with the Devil, though, because I have to take things in order, and both chronological order and the natural order of things demand that I begin with Paris and then proceed to the *femme fatale*. The latter element is the more important, because the key to everything that is of true literary interest—which is to say, love and death, especially in the aspects of passion and murder—can always be summed up by the French phase *cherchez la femme*. In this instance, however, *la femme* found me, and she first found me, although I was unaware of it at the time, in Paris.

Paris was, as it still is, the single most important sojourn that English youth made during the Grand Tour, of vital importance because it was there that Tourists learned to speak French fluently, and French was then the language most frequently spoken throughout continental Europe. France was also the spearhead of the Age of Enlightenment, the focal point of the intellectual *avant garde*, the location in which the seeds of a new world were sprouting in the rotten core of the old. More prosaically, it was a city replete with theaters, in which one could, if one were so inclined, see a different play performed almost every night.

I was so inclined; I was a glutton for theatrics. I was an exceedingly assiduous student of the theory and forms of contemporary playmaking, trying to learn as much as I could as quickly as I could, in order that I might carry it back with me to England and put it into practice, perhaps initially in Bristol, but ultimately in London.

Tragedy was still the most prestigious theatrical genre in Paris in 1786, and drama the up-and-coming "new genre," but I had a particular interest in comedy which naturally embraced a fascination with Molière, long dead but still a cardinal reference point for the French theater. While I was in Paris that fascination quickly extended to an interest in the new kinds of comedy that had been launched in Venice, recently imported to Paris by Carlo Goldoni, who had not only adapted many of his Italian plays into French but had begun writing new works in French.

During my sojourn in Paris there was a Venetian company that had taken up temporary residence in France, which performed plays in both French and Italian, and not only staged plays by Goldoni but by his rival and successor, Carlo Gozzi. I went to see at least half a dozen of those performances. I also interviewed the director of the troupe, Signor Landini, quite exhaustively, about the material he was importing and showcasing, and about its deep roots in the tradition of the *commedia dell'arte*—a tradition that had become almost as important in its manifestations on the French stage as it was in its native Italy.

Although she is not the *femme fatale* that I mentioned earlier, I ought to mention at this point in the story that it was at a performance of one of the Landini company's productions—a French adaptation of Gozzi's *Turandot*—that I first saw Adelaide Harrington. The second and third times that I saw her were also at the theater, and I realized that she must have an interest that, if not as obsessive as mine, must at least be very genuine. I nodded to her on the second occasion, and she returned the gesture of acknowledgement, before being reprimanded for so doing by the old lady accompanying her and serving as her chaperone.

After that, however, Adelaide and I continued to exchange more subtle acknowledgements, accompanied by knowing smiles, trying not to attract the lady's attention. By the time I discovered her name, and where she was staying in Paris, and Uncle Jerome had gathered a certain amount of information about her from other "bear-leaders" accompanying young men on the Tour and serving as their mentors, I considered that we already had a kind of conspiracy between us, and a common cause, even though we had not yet spoken to one another.

I will not say that I was already in love with Adelaide Harrington before my uncle and I left Paris, but I was certainly ready to fall in love with her, if an opportunity should present itself, and I was convinced that if and when an opportunity did crop up, she would not be averse to the prospect of a conversational meeting of minds, at the very least.

In those days, it was even rarer than it is now for young women to take the Grand Tour, despite the increasingly heavy emphasis that was being placed on the education of women. The kind of education that the Tour was supposed to provide, in broadening the mind by experience, was generally seen as something specifically suited to young men. Although the custom had spread from the aristocracy and landed gentry to the new generations of aspirant *nouveau riche* businessmen, to the extent that a Bristolian grandee of commerce like Archibald Bowlands felt compelled to send his sons and his grandson on the Tour, as an essential rung in climbing the social ladder, he would never have dreamed of sending either of my sisters or my female cousins.

Some of the custodians of older money, however, were not so backward in that kind of thinking, and Adelaide's father was evidently one of them. In allowing her to take the Tour, however, he had insisted that she be accompanied by a forceful chaperone, who gave a whole new significance to the term of "bear-leader" conventionally applied to members of the older generation who accompanied Tourists as educators and protectors, for she was indeed reminiscent of a she-bear in charge of a cub.

Perhaps unwisely, I had mentioned catching sight of Adelaide to

Uncle Jerome after the second glimpse, in terms that must have given away the attraction I felt toward her. He had immediately set out to discover who she was, and had soon contrived to obtain an introduction to the she-bear from one of the old hands who accompanied Tourists on a routine basis, Lord Kenavan.

The chaperone turned out, not unexpectedly, to be a maiden aunt, the sister of Adelaide's father. Uncle Jerome's attempt to liken her situation with regard to Adelaide to his with regard to me had not, however, been welcomed at all, and the elder Miss Harrington had made it abundantly clear to him that, given the alleged difference in our social standing— Adelaide's family belonged to the landed gentry of Kent while I was, in the old lady's scathing words "the scion of a pack of slave-traders"—it would be quite impossible for the two of us to meet socially. When Adelaide she left Paris, shortly before us, all that my uncle had been able to discover from his acquaintances about her future itinerary was that she intended to be in Venice for the Carnival early in the new year, as we also planned to be, along with many other Tourists who were leaving Paris and heading southwards before winter set in.

I feel that I ought to say, in passing, that my grandfather's association with the slave trade was exceedingly marginal, even though he was a dealer in cotton, much of which was undoubtedly cultivated by slaves. He had certainly never traded in slaves himself, although, as a native of Bristol and a man proud to style himself a "merchant adventurer," careless of the sometimes-euphemistic implications of the phrase, there might certainly have been grounds for considering him slightly guilty by association. He was no abolitionist, although my father and I both considered ourselves as belonging to the abolitionist camp in the contemporary debate.

That is, however, a minor matter; the real point of mentioning the episode, and Uncle Jerome's attempt to involve himself it, is that my relationships with the opposite sex, or lack of them, had become a slight bone of contention in the course of our Tour, since we had reached Paris. Although my uncle, slightly grudgingly, had sometimes agreed to accompany me on my theatrical excursions, I had stubbornly refused to accompany him on his occasional excursions to the brothels of the great French metropolis, sometimes in the company of other bear-leaders shepherding their young charges. He considered that not merely an inexcusable failure of reciprocity, but also a significant gap in my continuing "education," and his attempt to establish contact between me and Adelaide Harrington via her chaperone had been, in his eyes, a desperate attempt to pander to such interest in the fair sex as I had actually made manifest.

In fact, I had once gone to a brothel with Uncle Jerome, in Bristol, when I was seventeen, because my father, reluctant to undertake that particular parental duty himself, had been glad to entrust it to his brother, but I must confess that I had found the experience rather horrifying and well as somewhat degrading, and it had not been a habit that I ever had the slightest inclination to cultivate. My father, although he had not married young, had never been an assiduous client of whores himself, and was not in the least disapproving of my squeamishness, but my uncle, who, had adopted the custom with more enthusiasm, almost seemed to consider it a moral obligation, in his role as a Tour guide, to break through the barrier of what he considered to be my "prudishness."

I had ready excuses for my reluctance, of course—particularly the very real dangers of venereal disease—but my uncle tended to dismiss such concerns as evidence of an unmanly cowardice. He had continually assured me in Paris that Parisians whores were the most expert in the world, and that theirs was an art that no young man in search of a complete education ought to scorn, but he had not been able to sway me with that argument. Nor had he been able to persuade me with the other argument that he also put forward consistently, that the profession of actress was essentially a subcategory of whoredom and that no true theater lover ought to neglect that aspect of the obsession.

Those observations are also relevant to the attitude that Uncle Jerome adopted to my first encounter in Venice with the mysterious dark lady, and they go some way to explaining what might otherwise seem odd behavior on his part, unbefitting a serious mentor.

The hotel in which Uncle Jerome and I took lodgings when we arrived in Venice on the Friday before Shrove Tuesday—or Mardi Gras, in the more fashionable language of the Continent—was by no means the most fashionable in the city, being located not far from San Zan Degola in Santa Croce, nor was the apartment we acquired the best-appointed in the establishment. One of the penalties of arriving late at the generally-acknowledged climax of the Grand Tour, at the most fashionable time of year, is that most of the other Tourists get there ahead of you and take up all the best accommodation. Had we arrived two days later, we might well have been relegated to an attic in some decrepit edifice with a view over the lagoon limited on the horizon by one or other of the pestilential islets to which Tourists dare not go for fear of disease.

Mercifully, we were not reduced to that, and were able to find accommodation on the fourth floor of a rather imposing building overlooking one of the numerous subsidiary canals, whose main disadvantage was that it was distinctly gloomy for much of the day. There was, in fact, only an interval of a couple of hours, late in the afternoon, when the sun shone directly into the gap between the buildings from the west, not long before sunset, with brief intervals to either side, in the first of which the sun illuminated the facades opposite brightly while ours remained in the penumbra, while in the second, our facades obtained direct light and the other was shadowed. That shade would undoubtedly have been very welcome in the blaze of July, but Lent comes too early in the year for the heat and light to have become oppressive, and it began in mid-February in 1787.

On that first day, we arrived in the morning, and went out for a long and leisurely lunch before we began unpacking our trunks. By the time we had finished our meticulous organization, we were just entering the phase of daylight when the windows of our room were brightly and pleasantly sunlit, although the facades opposite were already becoming gloomily vague. When I went out on to the balcony in order to appreciate the view, therefore, the light had an odd chiaroscuro effect, which made it difficult for my eyes to adapt in order to make out the buildings on the other side of the canal with any degree of clarity.

Ordinarily, that would not have troubled me at all, and had my interest in those facades been purely architectural, the equivocal lighting would only have added to their charms. In fact, although it took me some time to realize the fact, there was a balcony almost directly opposite mine, on to which someone else emerged while I was standing on my own, and who inevitably drew my attention as soon as she had caught my eye, partly because she was a woman whose slim figure implied that she might be young, and perhaps beautiful, and partly because I could not dispel the suspicion that she was looking at me intently, perhaps even staring.

I was uncertain, of course, because she was masked.

There was nothing in the least unusual about that, because virtually everyone wears masks during the entire period of the Carnival of Venice, not merely in the evening but all day long. Nowadays, women who attend masked balls in London or Paris tend to wear what the French call *loups* and the Italians *Columbinas*, which cover the area around the eyes and the upper cheeks but leave the lower half of the face uncovered, but that is a relatively modern invention originating in the theater, favored by actresses because it allows them to declaim freely and reveal at least a fraction of their beauty. Earlier in the eighteenth century, the mask most commonly favored by patrician women during the Venetian carnival had been the *moretta muta*, which means "mute dark lady," and such masks had not fallen entirely out of fashion in 1787.

Although *moretta* masks had been largely replaced by the iconic *volta* or *larva*, usually white but sometimes decorated with gilt, which was a feminine variant of the masculine *volto*, many females still wore them. They retained a reputation for tastefulness because woman rarely wore the most grotesque carnival masks that men sometimes liked to sport, including the *bauta*, whose projecting lower section—designed to allow the wearer to eat and drink without unmasking—was greatly exaggerated in the beak of the much more bizarre *medico della pesta*.

There was, in consequence, nothing intrinsically astonishing in the fact that the lady on the balcony opposite mine was wearing a *moretta muta*. Some masks of that genre had relatively large eye-holes, which allowed the age of the wearer to be deducible by the degree of wrinkling around the eyes, but the one that the lady was wearing had small eye-holes that offered no such clue. All such masks covered the lower half of the face, so there was no clue to be obtained from the mouth and chin. By way of compensation, the mask did not obscure her luxurious long black hair, which helped to confirm the impression that she might be young, but was by no means a reliable indicator, Italian ladies often conserving glossy white hair even into their sixties.

The mere wearing of a less fashionable mask could not be reckoned reliable evidence of the wearer's age, so, in sum, I could not tell whether the woman I was looking at was twenty or sixty, or anywhere in between those extremes. The lady was clad in black, which was also far from unusual during the carnival, where long black cloaks and tricorn hats were standard accompaniments of the more familiar styles of mask, but the cloak draped over her shoulders was an abbreviated cape, whose hood was lowered, and over which her hair spilled, rather than the long cloak more frequently seen in the streets. The black dress she was wearing seemed to me, so far as I could judge in the dim light, to be more akin to mourning-dress than any kind of carnival costume, and my first inclination, on due reflection, was to wonder whether she might be a widow in mourning for a deceased husband, or a dutiful daughter mourning a deceased parent.

By far and away the most fascinating thing about her, from my point of view, however, was that she seemed to be looking at me so intently. I could not be absolutely sure of the fact, given the nature of the mask and the poor light, but that only added an edge of piquancy to the impression.

I was not unused to being the object of female gazes, and even of stares. I believe I can say without immodesty that when I was twenty-one I was an unusually handsome youth, although I thought at the time that the advantages of that were somewhat spoiled by the fact that I had the appearance of being some four or five years younger than I actually was, and had a somewhat effeminate appearance, greatly assisted by my fine and silky blond hair.

That appearance had been the bane of my life at school, where even boys who were younger than me were sometimes tempted to make an effort to bully me, and at Oxford, where I was the butt of continual gibes, sometimes in very poor taste. Being slimly-built had deterred me from attempting cultivate pugilistic skills as a form of self-defense, but I had taken up fencing, and acquired a certain amount of skill, and had often had occasion to regret that, even if I had been a gentleman in the stricter sense of the term, I no longer lived in an era when that rank would have qualified me to wear an épée in everyday society.

At twenty-one, as a member of adult society, those difficulties had mostly disappeared, but not entirely. In particular, the fashion in which young women of my own age tended to look at me and treat me tended to be a trifle condescending, if not actually tinged with contempt. Adelaide Harrington had been an exception in that regard, but a regrettably rare one. On the other hand—and it was an advantage for which I ought perhaps to have been far more grateful than I was—older women, tended to look at me in a much more kindly manner, sometimes quasi-maternally but, with perhaps surprising frequency, with a special character of quasi-nostalgic lust, as if I somehow represented lost opportunities of youth for which they now felt remorse.

Noticeable even in Bristol, where prim and stilted formality was the rule in all conventional interaction, that tendency had become particularly obvious in Parisian high society, where it had become a virtual cliché for aristocratic women in their forties deliberately to court much younger lovers, which they showed off in deliberate parody of the manner in which their middle-aged husband paraded their young mistresses. I had attracted a good deal of attention there, of which Uncle Jerome naturally advised me to take full advantage—but I had refused, just as adamantly as I refused his entreaties to sample the city's brothels. I only had eyes for the distant, and seemingly forever-out-of-reach, Adelaide.

Because of that experience, the fact that the masked woman on the balcony opposite mine seemed to be staring at me appraisingly—which, I was well aware, might itself by an illusion—also cast doubt on the impression I had of her youth. I could not help but wonder whether she might be considerably older than my initial hopeful appraisal had suggested.

Had I been wearing a mask, I would probably have looked back more intently and more inquisitively, one of the great advantages of carnival masks being that they cover up the ostentation of a stare, but for the purposes of unpacking my luggage I had taken off the *volto* that I had worn when I went to lunch, and which I intended to wear outside the hotel for the duration of the carnival, when I went out into the streets to mingle with the general celebration, or went to the theater, as I hoped to do every night. Although I was fully-dressed from the neck down, therefore, I was very conscious of my naked face and the effective disadvantage in which it placed me relative to the dark lady. I felt that I could not stare at her in the fashion in which I suspected that she was staring at me, for fear of seeming horribly impolite—all the more so as my face was still brightly lit by sunlight, while hers was in shadow.

I therefore pretended, in what must have been a woefully unconvincing fashion, to be taking in the entire view, looking to the left and the right, and down toward the water of the canal, where the occasional gondola was gliding over the suspiciously oily and rather malodorous surface, even while my mental attention and my intense curiosity were focused entirely on her.

How long the mute confrontation lasted I cannot be sure, but it was only a matter of minutes. Just before the sun slipped behind the edge of the block of buildings opposite, however and the shadow reached across the gap to consume my balcony as well as hers, she raised a black-gloved hand to her moretta, where it covered her mouth, and blew me a strangely languorous, and—or so it seemed to me—fervently amorous kiss.

Immediately afterwards, the sun was eclipsed. I suppose that must have required several seconds, at least, but I was so dazed by the unexpected gesture that I was hardly aware of any transition. There was the kiss, and then there was a blurring grayness that made me doubt, not the fact of it but the impression it had made on me. Surely, I thought the kiss could not have been as amorous as it seemed?

Even in the absence of direct sunlight, it was still daylight, but it seemed as if I had been plunged into sudden obscurity, and that the black-clad form that was already ill-defined had disappeared into the gloom and had been swallowed up. By the time my eyes had adapted to the lower light intensity and I could once again make out the wrought iron railings of the opposite balcony clearly, the location was empty. The woman had presumably stepped back into the room behind her, and had drawn the shutters closed as soon as she was inside.

II

UNCLE JEROME'S OPINIONS

I turned around and went back into the sitting room of our own apartment just as Uncle Jerome collapsed heavily into an armchair, saying: "At last!"

In the twenty-some years since he had taken the Grand Tour for the first time, in the protective company of his brother and a "bear-leader" of their own, my uncle had changed a great deal, physically as well as mentally. When he had leapt at the opportunity that my father had offered him to serve as my guide, he had doubtless thought of the voyage as an attempt to recapture his youth, but he had discovered long before we reached Switzerland that his youth was irrecoverable, in many of its most important aspects. He remembered his younger self, perhaps not entirely accurately, as having been essentially untiring, but his forty-seven years now rendered him far more vulnerable to exhaustion. The excursions we had undertaken in the Alps had more than once reduced his legs to jelly, and as for the whoring expeditions to which he had been so looking forward...well, to put it kindly, they had provided a stern challenge to what he insisted on calling, in what seemed to me to be a rather quaint fashion, his "sap."

While socializing with other bear-leaders in Paris, my uncle had found others in a similar situation, including a Yorkshireman named Heckenfield, a mill-owner who had done business with Bowlands and Sons, who must have been one of the first of his ilk to take the Tour, and had likewise sought to recover its magic by acting as mentor to a nephew of his own. He too had been disappointed, although he and my father had both been buoyed up by the imperishable bonhomie of Lord Kenavan, who had made the Tour repeatedly, perhaps as many as a dozen times, having effectively become a professional bear-leader, accompanying the scions, in groups of three or more, of half of the aristocratic families who divided their social lives between Mayfair and the shires. In consequence, he had become a guides' guide, educating less experienced peers not only in the science of bear-leading but in the kinds of endurance required by the middle-aged in traipsing round Europe.

In spite of that advice, however, Uncle Jerome was beginning to find the wear and tear of incessant travel distinctly arduous, and the prospect of a sojourn in Venice that would extend for at least a week, and perhaps longer, was understandably pleasing, offering a promise of abundant relaxation.

"Why the long face?" he asked me, as I came back into the room, presumably with an expression slightly clouded with puzzlement.

"Is the building directly opposite, on the far side of the canal, a hotel or a private house?" I asked him.

"How the hell should I know?" he replied. "Does it matter?"

"Probably not," I admitted. "It's just that there was a woman on the opposite balcony who seemed to be staring at me."

"Possibly because you aren't wearing a mask," he suggested, "and she thought you were improperly dressed. Was she young or old?"

"I don't know. She was wearing a *moretta*. She…" I hesitated, wondering how much I ought to reveal, and settled for discretion. "I had an odd feeling that she might have recognized me, and I couldn't help wondering whether she actually lived in the apartment, or whether she might be a Tourist, on the same circuit as us."

"Oh, God," he groaned. "You think it might be that chit with whom you became distantly besotted in Paris, don't you? I wish I'd never made enquiries on your behalf now. Even if she has come to Venice for the carnival, as planned, the chances are that you won't see her, and even if you do, you won't recognize her because she'll be masked, and even if you did recognize her, you'd only be able to moon after her at a distance, as you did there."

I was annoyed by his jumping to that conclusion, partly because it was not entirely incorrect, even though I knew full well how absurd it was to make an immediate imaginative connection between that solemnly blown kiss and the nods and smiles I had exchanged with Adelaide Harrington in Paris. I knew that Uncle Jerome had renewed his hopes for my recruitment to the cause of licentiousness as we approached Venice, because he had already waxed lyrical about the allure of masks in "gallant courtship." Given that, I thought I ought to respond dismissively to the comment he had made in response to my remark about the masked woman on the opposite balcony.

"Oh no," I said. "It certainly wasn't Adelaide or anyone similar. The lady on the balcony had beautiful black hair, of a kind one very rarely sees in England, and she was dressed entirely in black—but whether that signifies that she's in mourning, I don't know. Given that there are so many people in the streets who seem to be dressed as *memento mori*,

I suppose it might simply be an affectation."

"And that look attracts you, does it?" he enquired, with the gleam in his eye of a man who had just glimpsed a possibility.

"No," I told him, sternly, "but in this instance, it intrigued me. As I said, the lady seemed to be staring at me, and I couldn't help wondering why—although it might have been an illusion, given that she was standing in shadow and wearing a *moretta*. Perhaps she was simply staring into space, contemplatively…which, if she really has suffered a recent loss, might be understandable."

"I might also make it more understandable that she mistook you for an angel," Uncle Jerome observed, a trifle sarcastically. It was a standard joke on his part, encouraged by the attention I had attracted in Paris from those Roman Catholic ladies "of a certain age," who frequently favored personal adornments in the form of crucifixes and sometimes disguised what was probably just restless fidgeting as the pious telling of rosary beads. If I had had a guinea for every time some Parisian dowager had referred to me as her *"bel ange"*—Parisian ladies are very casual in the matter of compliments—I could have financed that phase of my Grand Tour without any assistance from grandfather's coffers.

"Perhaps she did," I said, deciding that it was probably best to enter into the joke. "Blond hair and a rosy complexion like mine probably seem a trifle exotic to Venetians, in spite of the geographical proximity of the Tyrol, where there's certainly no shortage of them. Once I put on my *larva* in order to go out, though, the illusion will probably disappear." I used that alternative term for the standard mask, signifying "ghost," in preference to *volto*, which simply means "face," deliberately.

"Personally," he said, "I shall wear a *bauta*, so that I can drink more easily. It's more traditional, too."

"Not a *medico della peste?*" I suggested.

He shook his head vehemently. "Now that, I don't understand," he said. "Why people should want to wander round looking like skeletal storks is beyond me. I know that they're supposed to ward off disease, but even if it were true, they're simply too ludicrous. I suppose you've already made your plans for tonight? I saw you when we went for lunch, peering at theaters. How many handbills did you collect from clowns?"

"They're Pierrots," I told him. "We're in Venice now, where we really must use the proper terms for the archetypes of the commedia." Whether it was a long tradition for Venetian theaters to employ actors costumed as Pierrot to distribute their publicity material to Tourists or simply a brief fad, I had no idea, but Uncle Jerome's observation had a certain justice to it. I had collected half a dozen playbills, all of them from Pierrots, who were difficult to tell apart even though Pierrot traditionally wears white make-up rather than a *volto*, and individuals in the relevant costume inevitable differ in stature and build.

"Yes, I have made my plans," I confirmed. "So have you, I imagine."

"You're going to the theater, I suppose?"

"Indeed."

He sighed. "Is your Italian really up to following the dialogue?"

"I hope so. In any case, the costumes will all be recognizable, as the same stock characters are so abundantly used in France, and much of the comedy will be visual."

"You're going to see a comedy, then? Not one of the tragedies you liked so much in Paris?"

"Italy has a very different theatrical tradition, especially Venice, and especially during the Carnival. Comedy is dominant here, albeit sometimes tinged in black. You should come with me—you might enjoy it more than the tragedies you sat through in such a long-suffering manner in Paris."

"Absolutely not. French I can follow well enough, but I get lost trying to keep up with Italian, I'm not as familiar as you are with stock characters, and physical humor leaves me cold. I'll be quite content with a glass of wine in a tavern on the Piazza San Marco, watching the world go by."

"Looking out for Mr. Heckenfield, no doubt, and the senior shepherd."

"They should be here," he replied, refusing to object to my description of Lord Kevanan, "and I promised them in Paris that I'd meet up with them here. They must be wondering where I've got to."

"Blame me," I said, "and my desire to scale more mountains than the standard itinerary recommends."

"I will," he promised. "You really ought to spend at least one leisurely evening on the Piazza. It's a theatrical performance in itself, with everyone in fancy dress—it's one of the most striking memories I've retained of my own tour. With luck, as you say, I'll be able to meet up with some of the friends I made in Paris, and you have no reason to be contemptuous of them. Kenevan is exceedingly good company, as well as knowing everything there is to know about the stages of the tour. He was very useful in Paris, and his advice will be invaluable to us in Venice."

"Just be careful not to play cards with him. He gives me the impression of being a sharper, and the only wager I'd be willing to lay in his vicinity is that his title isn't to be found in Burke's *Peerage*."

"Snobbery doesn't suit you, Gabriel. You might not be the scion of pirates and slave-traders, as the worthy Miss Harrington thinks, but you're a cotton merchant by ancestry, even if you're a playwright by vocation."

I repented of my sarcasm, which had been prompted by the residual unease inspired by the blown kiss. "Sorry, Uncle," I said. "Shall I come to look for you in the Piazza after the performance? If you do manage to link up with a gang of Englishmen, you'll be easy enough to spot, even if you're all wearing *bautas*."

"There'll be more than one such group," he assured me. "The Grand Tour is so popular nowadays, and the Carnival of Venice such a key reference point, that you can hear far more English spoken in the city than French, and most of the natives have at least a mattering of the language. In any case, the Piazza will be far too crowded, and you'll never recognize me at a distance if I'm on my own. I'll meet you back here. I certainly won't be too late back. I'm tired after that long sprint through Lombardy, and I need a good night's sleep in a real bed."

"I'll try not to disturb you if I come in late," I said, although it was not a serious danger. Once Uncle Jerome started snoring, it would have required a gunshot to wake him.

The play that I went to see that night was the last of the comedies written in Italian by Goldoni, *Gil amori de Zelinda e Lindoro*, which was already more than a decade old. Rumor alleged that Goldoni had been "driven out" of Venice after quarreling with his great rival Carlo Gozzi, who had stayed to become the dominant presence in Venetian theater, but Goldoni was still greatly respected there and his works were always in performance, especially during the Carnival. Among the two, I had a distinct preference for Gozzi, especially with his respect to his folklore-based fantasies, which I was especially keen to investigate further and examine more closely, but I thought it best to take in the Goldoni first, if only for the purposes of comparison and contrast.

I did find the dialogue in the play very difficult to follow, but it would not have helped very much had I had the opportunity to study a printed version beforehand, as I had sometimes been able to do in Paris. Venetian comedy had supposedly moved on considerably from the ancient forms of the *commedia dell'arte*, but it had retained a good deal of the tradition of improvisation, by which standardized characters moved through routine of interaction and conflict, but varied the routines, especially their oral component, in order to satirize recent events and adapt to the reaction of particular audiences. On the other hand, it was the working of that process that I particularly wanted to study, so I found the performance fascinating, even though I could not pretend to follow it in every detail.

The audience in the theater seemed particularly bizarre, by comparison with audiences in Paris. Only a handful were wearing full costumes of the kind that would doubtless be seen in far greater abundance in the Piazza and along the Grand Canal, but everyone was masked, and although *voltos* and *voltas* were in the great majority, there were a considerable number of *bautas* mimgled with them, more than a few *morettas* and even the occasional *medico della peste*. The overall effect of that vast parade of hidden faces was strangely overwhelming, perhaps more so in juxtaposition with somber clothing than with the more colorful attire favored during daylight hours.

I would have scanned the boxes carefully in any case, simply to drink on the panorama, but I now had two extra reasons for doing so, albeit ones that seemed a trifle absurd. As well as the faint hope that I might see Adelaide Harrngton in the audience, and that she might recognize my golden hair and favor me with a slyly impertinent nod of the head, I could not help fantasizing that I might catch a glimpse of a raven-haired woman clad entirely in black, who might respond to a similar recognition by blowing me a kiss.

Nothing of the sort happened, of course, and I chided myself for my imbecility—although, looking back over the distance of decades, and still in doubt as to the exact nature of my adventure, I cannot help wondering whether, in fact, I did already have an inkling of the fact that I was caught up in something exceedingly strange.

As I walked back to the hotel after the performance, the multitudinous lanterns in the streets and along the canals, reflected from so many white masks, made it very evident indeed why the *volto* and its feminine counterpart were also known by the title of *larvae*. Venice during the Carnival did indeed resemble a city of ghosts, populated by the ambulant dead, and the occasional beaks of the *medico della peste*, also ivory white, seemed positive supernatural amid so many flickering flames. It was not, however, reminiscent of Hell, at least in my imagination. Heaven it was definitely not, but I could not imagine it as Purgatory either. The Venetian *commedia* was outside the scope of the Dantean *Comedia*, belonging to another world, or at least another world-view, devoid of demons and angels alike—or so it seemed that first night, before subsequent encounters began to modify the imagination of my mind's eye.

Uncle Jerome must have been just as tired as he thought, because he was already in bed, and snoring in his most sonorous fashion, by the time I got back to the hotel, and I did not get the chance to talk to him, either about my experience at the theater and walking home through the streets, or his in some wine-shop, watching the hectic life of the piazza—although I doubt that ether of us felt that we had missed anything important in consequence.

III

THE INVITATION

Much of the following day, we spent together, exploring the city at what seemed to me to be an exceedingly leisurely pace. My uncle took his role as cicerone very seriously, and planned an elaborate itinerary taking in the greater number of the standard Tourist shrines, dutifully setting foot in all six *sestieri* as well as gliding along the Grand Canal and some of the other popular waterways. The architectural marvels were impressive, but began to blur somewhat in spite of the slow pace at which we traveled from one to the next.

The idea of the excursion was to give me a general idea of the city, in order that we could then select out items for more elaborate and more detailed examination on subsequent days, but I was somewhat dazed by the complexity of the waterways and the labyrinthine streets, and I found it difficult to draw up any kind of list that might form the basis of a timetable—except, of course, for carefully taking note of the position of various theaters, and collecting information from numerous playbills—a focusing of effort that caused my uncle to frown more than once.

"They're actually coming too seek you out," he said of one Pierrot, who had woven a way through a crowd to hand me a small sheet of paper. "Mask or no mask, your hair and the cut of your clothes gives you away. They already know that you're a star customer, and they're competing for your attention."

"You're exaggerating," I told him. "Perhaps it is obvious that I'm English, but I hardly think that I can have acquired any notoriety. We've only been here a little over twenty-four hours, and it's not as if the name of Bowlands means anything here, in spite of the volume of cotton that's gone into all those fancy costumes."

"You acquired a measure of notoriety in Paris," Uncle Jerome observed, "if only as an imitation angel, and the acquaintances we made there among the Tourists have mostly preceded us here."

"You met Mr. Heckenfield last night, then?" I asked "And Kenavan too?"

"Yes. They were oddly glad to see me, for which I suppose I ought to be flattered—but Kenavan asked after you with even more enthusiasm, it seemed to me."

"Really?" I said. "He's your friend, not mine—I hardly exchanged a dozen words with him."

"He says he's sure that you'll be just as much of a success with the ladies here as you were there. Apparently, he didn't realize that you were squandering all your opportunities."

"Judging me by himself, no doubt," I said. "He probably cut quite a swathe through middle-aged Marquises and Comtesses when he was my age. Too old for it now, though."

"To judge by the stories he tells, he did and he still does," my uncle replied, more than a trifle enviously, "but one always has to take tales of that sort with a pinch of salt."

"One certainly does," I said. "Didn't you tell me that he claims to know both Mesmer and Cagliostro, and dabbles in fashionable occultism himself?"

"Oh, that's just for show."

"And playing Don Juan isn't?"

"Well, perhaps. Who can blame him, if it is? Better than playing Don Quixote or Galahad."

"That's a matter of opinion," I told him.

It wasn't until we stopped for lunch, in the vicinity of Santi Giovanni e Paolo in Castello, that my uncle mentioned, with contrived casualness: "I made enquiries about the mystery woman on the balcony opposite while you were out last night, by the way?"

I felt a quasi-electric shock, but I tried to affect the most utter indifference.

"Really?" I said. "Of whom?"

"The hotel staff, of course. Hotel staff always know everything—or can always find out in a matter of hours."

"And?"

"The building on the far side of the canal is divided into private apartments. The one on the fourth floor was occupied until recently by a reclusive minor aristocrat who died last year. Apparently, he left a widow much younger than himself, so there's a possibility that the woman you saw really was dressed in mourning. The hotel clerk didn't know much about her, except that she's a Florentine, who was only in Venice sporadically for three or four years, and spent most of her time here in the apartment, rarely going out, even to church. She's said to be beautiful, but I couldn't get a more detailed description, an accurate estimate of her age, or even a Christian name. Her husband's name was Giacomo Senedese, though, and he was said to be the descendant of a family once prominent in Murano." As a dutiful Tour guide, he added: "That's an island-complex in the lagoon about a mile beyond the northern shore of Venice proper."

I had already heard of Murano, the center of the legendary Venetian glass industry, and intended to visit it when I could.

"If it really was her," I said, "It might be the blond angels of Florentine Renaissance art for which she feels nostalgic. Perhaps, struck by the last rays of direct sunlight before the shadow claimed me, I reminded her of an image depicted by Giotto or Botticelli."

I was improvising; my tour had not yet reached Florence, whereas Uncle Jerome had been there, but I suspected that his memory of the artistic legacy of Lorenzo the Magnificent was overshadowed by rose-tinted memories of the city's prostitutes. He knew enough about artistic tradition, however, to reply: "Given that many of the figures mistaken for angels by pious tourists are actually *amore*," he said, "you might be misinterpreting the nature of her interest yourself."

In view of the memory of the blown kiss, that gibe struck more poignantly than he had intended.

We headed back to the hotel once we had eaten, partly because the walking was beginning to take its toll on Uncle Jerome's feet and partly because I intended to catch a performance of Carlo Gozzi's *Il Mostro Turchino* that started earlier than was customary, presumably in order to catch the crowd before the company's rivals. We walked very slowly, taking a slightly roundabout route in order to embrace an extra ration of architecture, but Uncle Jerome's commentary had definitely suffered a considerable diminution of verve and enthusiasm. I appreciated the relaxation, because it gave my attention more scope to wander, to take in the true bizarrerie of the masked population thronging the city, on land and water alike.

But they're all acting, I thought. *The native population is actually in a minority at this time of year, and even the true Venetians who remain, mingling with the Tourists who are playing their roles so enthusiastically, are similarly putting on a show. The Carnival is partly scripted and partly improvised, but it no longer has any spontaneity or authenticity. It has become self-parody, a fantastic comedy in its own right, clearly reflecting the long and irrevocable decline in the city's economic and political fortunes as patterns of trade shift and processes of manufacture are transformed.*

As we came past the office adjacent to the vestibule of the hotel, a clerk hastened out to hand me a sealed letter, addressed in what looked like feminine handwriting to *Signor Gabriel Bowlands*.

"How did this arrive?" I asked.

"Messenger," sad the clerk tersely.

"But how can anyone know that I'm here?" I wondered.

The clerk shrugged.

"Has anyone been asking about us?" Uncle Jerome put in—but all he got in reply to that was a nod, and he obviously did not feel that his command of the Italian language, especially in its peculiar Venetian dialect, was adequate to a more elaborate inquisition.

I trudged up four flights of stairs and waited for my uncle to open the door of our room before I broke the seal on the envelope and took out the single sheet of paper that it contained.

The unsigned note was neatly written in English, but its relative terseness and the slightly exaggerated clarity with which the letters were formed might have been construed as evidence that English was not the writer's first language.

It read:

> *If you are chivalrous and adventurous, Signor Gabriel, be in the square of San Giacomo dell'Orio at midnight, and follow the man who comes to you.*

I showed it to Uncle Jerome, who laughed delightedly. "It seems that your masked beauty really was staring at you, but that she mistook you for an *amore* and not an angel after all."

"But it's unsigned," I complained. "It could have come from anyone."

"Nonsense," he replied. "If ever there was an invitation to a covert amorous rendezvous, that's definitely one, and who could possibly have any interest in making such an approach so mysteriously, except for a widow in mourning careful of propriety? Who else could possibly have sent it?"

I made no reply, and he read far more into my silence than was actually there to read.

"You think your blessed Adelaide might be trying to avoid the surveillance of her dragon? Don't be ridiculous. You haven't even caught sight of her."

There was no need for any contradiction, because my conviction was identical to his, but I couldn't help reacting to his tone of scorn.

"Not knowingly," I said. "But *volto* or not, as you've already pointed out, I'm easily recognizable for anyone who's seen me before by virtue of my hair, and just as we were informed that the Harringtons planned to be here for the Carnival, Adelaide could easily have been informed that we were aiming for the same objective."

"And do you honestly think that the daughter of some petty Kentish squire would address a note like that to a man she's only glimpsed— even a man who looks like a pubescent angel?"

"No," I admitted. "But I have equal difficulty in thinking that the widow of a Venetian aristocrat would address it to an obvious Tourist that she'd only glimpsed for a matter of seconds across the width of a canal."

"You're unfamiliar with continental mores," said Uncle Jerome, loftily. "Given the way that some of those Parisian matrons looked at you, I'm surprised that you didn't accumulate a boxful of notes like that before we left France, although I suppose the city's boldest predators were all lying in ambush in Versailles. On the other hand, simply because Miss Harrington was the only woman in Paris who caught your unduly selective eye, it doesn't mean that you didn't catch the eye of some other English traveler who found out very easily that you would be in Venice for the Carnival and has spent a month and more brooding over future amorous possibilities while you were studying glaciers in the Alps. My money is still on the dark lady on the balcony, though. Notes of that kind are a continental amorous tradition, not an English one."

"There isn't any explicit reference in the note to an amorous rendezvous," I said.

"Well, of course not—such things aren't stated explicitly. Do you think it's some kind of trap, then? Do you want me to go in your stead? Although, as you say, it's your hair that makes you recognizable, and I can't simulate that. Anyway, we wouldn't want to disappoint the lady, would we? If she's hungry for tender meat, she won't settle for a gamy old bird like me."

"But…" I began.

"Oh, come on, Gabriel," he said. "If you're scared of being beaten and robbed, don't take any money with you, and take advantage of the fact that everyone's in costume to strap on your blessed rapier. God, when I was your age I wouldn't have hesitated for a moment to answer a summons like that, had I been fortunate enough to receive one. What have you got to lose, damn it—not your virginity; I know that for a fact! Given that you're too precious to consort with whores and too timorous to get within touching distance of the likes of Adelaide Harrington, why not take advantage of the opportunities you do have? You've already admitted that you were...how did you put it?...*intrigued*. You wondered why she seemed to be staring at her; now you know. You also know the items of information that I took the trouble to find out for you, so you're not walking into the situation completely blind."

"If it's her," I objected, stubbornly.

"*If*," he mocked. "Well, what if it isn't? Either way, it's an adventure. And that's the challenge it's offering you, isn't it? Are you adventurous, or are you going to be content to sit in the audience for the rest of your life, watching the actresses play their allotted roles, content to look and admire but never to touch?"

I remember thinking at the time that Uncle Jerome was the person who was supposed to be guiding me on my Tour, meanwhile making sure that no harm came to me. In his eyes, however, the supervision of my education did not stop, or even begin, with monuments and works of art, and the most important mountains to be scaled and rivers to be crossed were the metaphorical ones.

In the end, I shrugged my shoulders, and said: "All right—why not?"

"I'm sure the lady will be grateful for your enthusiasm," said Uncle Jerome. "Just remember that you're a Bowlands, and that the family honor is at stake, if not the entire reputation of the Merchant Adventurers of Bristol."

"I'll bear it in mind," I assured him, sourly, as I set off for the performance of *Il Mostro Turchino*.

As I walked through the streets, where dusk was just beginning to fall, I was struck once again by the seeming apathy of the performing crowds, who no longer seemed to me to be wearing their costumes with any real degree of enthusiasm or conviction. If the whole city were to be reckoned a stage, and all the people in it merely players, they now seemed distinctly weary of their roles. Perhaps it was an effect of the fading light, or perhaps a reflection of my changed mood, not so much because of having received the mysterious invitation to adventure but because of my uncle's reaction to it.

I tried to shake off the mood and the impression by assuring myself that the comedy was sure to liven up again, if not the following day—which was Sunday—but surely when Shrove Tuesday actually arrived, that being a day of supposedly-unparalleled festivity. Apart from the falling dusk, I reminded myself, the entire city was effectively in suspension, with the opening phases of the long celebration already over but the climax not yet in sight, and perhaps too long delayed. The extravagance that was on display at present inevitably rang false, and the ostentatious pleasure-seeking represented by the costumes and the masks was marking time, as a vulgar matter of course—but that was only temporary.

Or was it?

Given my general frame of mind, I couldn't help wondering whether what I was seeing in that brief phase of twilight was a reality partially hidden by the glare of broad daylight and the mask of night alike. Perhaps, I thought, it was only at dusk that the Decadence of Venice was really displayed in its naked lassitude and decrepitude, showing not merely its age but its obsolescence.

In Venice, I knew by virtue of my preliminary research, the most important festival of the year was the fortnight after Ascension Day, when the golden ship *Bucentaur* carried the doge from his palace to cast the betrothal-ring of the Republic into the sea, in order symbolically to seal the sacred bargain that had maintained the city's wealth and power for a thousand years. Then, too, masks were worn, and the city donned all its finery. Second in importance, in the years when the election of a new doge did not license a special fête, was St Mark's Day. Even Shrove Tuesday was, at best, no more significant than Christmas, albeit more elaborately anticipated because the weather was milder and the twilight later. As for the days beforehand, perhaps it was foolish of the Venetians to retain them as part of the celebration, given that the pace of social life had accelerated so rapidly in recent decades. Perhaps it was time even for Venice to limit its celebration of the *carne vale*, the farewell to meat before the Lenten fast, to a single day, to focus all its theatrical effort on the comedy of Mardi Gras, "fat Tuesday," itself.

I reflected, as my gaze swept over all the masked faces, that Uncle Jerome had been promising me for weeks me a riot of pomp and pleasure that would exhaust the strongest mind and stomach in the continent; but from what I had seen so far in Venice, it was more a ripple than a riot. The residents of the city, inured by long experience, did not present any evidence of surfeit, and I was skeptical that three more days would succeed in driving them to excess. The Tourists and other visitors seemed to be summoning up a more determined will, but the will in question was slightly feverish, as if haunted by a strange kind of anxiety and bewilderment. The subterfuges of *ennui* were being stoutly resisted by the city's visitors, but it seemed to me that there was a kind of desperation in that resistance.

You have doubtless heard of Venice as a liquid city, where gondolas play the part of carriages on arterial highways, but when the Carnival was in full flow in those days the water of the Grand Canal almost disappeared beneath a motley dress of barges and feluccas, galleys and skiffs, whose helmsmen were perennially cursing one another for impeding their progress. All of the vessels were decorated with paint and colored cloth, as if they were costumed and masked in the same manner as the people and the booths crowding the Piazza San Marco, but they were huddled together in evident discomfort, and the overriding impression was not one of joy or splendor, but of impatience and stasis.

The crowds in the Piazza, the Piazzetta and the Mole extended like the coils of a snake around the multitudinous stalls and booths set up there, where goods of every kind were sold, fortunes told by every method known to superstition, all manner of freaks, prodigies and exotic animals displayed, and performances mounted by musicians, acrobats and clowns, but as I passed through the heart of the city on that particular occasion, on my way to see *Il Mostro Turchino*, the overwhelming impression created in me by the entire scene was steeped in the ambivalence of the twilight, abandoned by the sun but not yet ready to combat the dark with defiant flame.

I tried to shake off the bleak echo in my soul by telling myself that the lassitude and falsity of the spectacle, even if it persisted, was irrelevant to my particular purpose for being there. Yes, I had been brought to Venice by the natural desire to see one of Christendom's finest cities and only great republic, and to see the Carnival of Venice in all its gaudy glory, but those were very general ambitions, merely standard elements of the syllabus of the Grand Tour. What was personal to me, and dear to my own heart, was the opportunity to see performances of works by Carlo Goldoni and Carlo Gozzi, the two contrasted masters of the new Venetian comedy, and also to discover the new writers who were benefiting from the artistic revolution they had wrought and would doubtless carry it even further.

The transformation they had wrought was, however, limited. All the characters of the Commedia were still in Venice, not merely in the theatres where Goldoni's and Gozzi's plays were being performed in a formal manner, but on the water and the land alike. They had broken free from their former servitude in becoming models for four in every five of the fanciful costumes that the low-ranking Venetians put on in order to enjoy their festival, and as I walked through the focal point of the city's cultural life I was literally surrounded by Arlecchinos and Pierrots, Brighellas and Scaramuccias, Columbinas and Pantalones. Such copies and pastiches had become the common uniform of hawkers, barkers and street-performers, but they were ever-present in the crowds too, no matter where I looked. Venice in the 1780s was full of new and eminently fashionable theatres, but on carnival days the whole city became a theatre of phantoms, relics of theatrical times past.

Seen in that light, as a phantom of the old Commedia, the tiredness and the tawdriness did not seem so offensive to me. I told myself—and believed it—that there is a magnificence even in exhaustion and fakery, if one only cares to ennoble it by construing such labels as Decadence as marks of esthetic appreciation rather than insults. That was what I tried to do as the natural light faded away completely and the light of lanterns gradually increased in volume to replace and transfigure it. Lamplight, as I had scrupulously observed the previous evening, has a power of transformation which can seem magical, if one can only find the right frame of mind in which to view it.

"Every action is dramatic, after all," I murmured, "and no matter how dispirited the performance seems, the important thing here and now is that no one can tell where the audience ends and the players begin, or when the comedy ends and the tragedy begins."

There was no point, I thought, in regretting that the present phase of the Carnival of Venice lacked energy; for a playmaker like me that very lack to energy ought merely to be a kind of comedy, a satirical reflection.

And hindsight now confirms that I was surely right. Venice then must have been closely akin to what Rome must have been in the days of the Syrian princes, which some French scholars were beginning to call the Latin Decadence and others an Age of Madness. Doubtless the city's morality left much to be desired, even from the viewpoint of an England that had not yet glimpsed the possibility of the advent of Queen Victoria, but what I saw as I walked its streets on that Saturday was not a city in the grip of the traditional seven deadly sins, but a city in the grip of a single anomalous sin, the particular kind of *ennui* that Medieval Christians called *accidie*: a city tired even of wickedness and appealing for release, not with heroism, but nevertheless with a certain languid style.

That was the mood in which I went into the theater to watch Gozzi's comedy, and that was the frame of mind in which I watched it. I found it much harder to follow that the Goldoni play, which had been more carefully structured, with fewer musical interludes and whimsical improvisations, but in several ways it was more rewarding, simply because of its fantastic nature. Then as now, there were many so-called philosophers—in the English sense of the word—who took it for granted that in an Age of Enlightenment the apparatus of superstition ought to disappear from human thought, being reduced to mere nonsense unworthy of intellectual attention. Goldoni pandered to that assumption to a large extent in his rigorously naturalistic comedies, but Gozzi had a very different attitude, finding the implausible and the ridiculous an exceedingly rich source of comedy, not least because its non-sense, in undermining the arrogant assumptions of common sense, showed up their crudity and frailty.

I liked the play greatly, perhaps because rather than in spite of the fact that I could not quite grasp it. When it was over, and I began the long walk back to San Croce, I initially set my course, unthinkingly, for the hotel, but as I walked, looking about me at the half-hearted fading, tokenistic manifestations of the festival, which now seem even more ghostly in the phantasmagorical lighting, I decided that I did not want to go back there in the interim before midnight.

I knew that I would not find my uncle asleep this time, and that I would have to face the renewal of his sniping, with regard to the alleged amorous rendezvous to which I had been invited. It would do no good to tell him that I had decided to go to it; he would not believe it until he saw me set forth and even then would not believe that I was actually going where I was bid, and that I would actually follow the man who came to collect me, if anyone did.

I decided, in consequence, to avoid the hotel, and to kill time by wandering the streets until the moment came when I would actually have to make the crucial decision, and go, or not.

Because Venice is a network of islands, it is virtually impossible to get lost there—or, to put it more accurately, although it is exceedingly easy to get lost there if you are visiting the city for the first time, it is also very easy, once you are lost, to find your bearings again, simply by walking until you reach the Grand Canal or the shore of the lagoon. I therefore walked somewhat at random, albeit maintaining a vaguely westerly direction, in order that I would end up somewhere in San Croce, within a stone's throw of San Giacomo dell'Orio, which I had every confidence in my being able to locate.

For that reason, I could not say the day after, and certainly cannot say now, exactly where it was that I stumbled over the Devil, except that it was in an ill-lit and narrow by-way within earshot of the campanile of San Giacomo dell'Orio. I never saw it again, and I sometimes wonder whether it was a real street at all, or a kind of sidestep away from the world, into some nether region into which common mortals normally cannot, and perhaps should not, stray.

IV

THE DEVIL UNMASKED

When I say that I "stumbled over" the Devil I mean it literally, not metaphorically. I could not see the ground over which I was walking, and although I was treading carefully, I was nevertheless caught out by the recumbent body, and almost went sprawling. Fortunately, I managed to catch myself in time, and retain my upright stance, after a certain windmilling of the arms.

I had a stub of candle in my pocket, and a briquette, with the aid of which I managed to light it, and what I saw brought an instinctive gasp of alarm, not so much because of the costume that the supine form was wearing as the suspicion that it might be a corpse. In fact, the Devil gave the impression that he might well have been unconscious before I collided with him—but once I had lit the candle, he did not take long to stir, and then to groan.

He was not the first Devil I had seen that day, although such costumes were far less common in the Commedia-dominated Venetian Carnival than they are nowadays in Parisian Opéra balls, where Princes of Hell are almost as commonplace as Princes of the Blood. He was, however, a particularly grotesque Devil, not so much because of his horns and the black greasepaint liberally smeared in his face by way of a fluid mask as because of the strangely convincing tail coiled up beneath him, the fake cloven hooves into which he had squeezed his feet and the clawed gloves in the form of feline paws into which he had compressed his hands. His body was covered in a kind of shaggy red leotard, with dark streaks, and lying on the ground beside him beside him was a trident with steel-tipped prongs.

It was only on closer inspection, when I knelt down with the candle-stub, that I noticed that the material forming the core of his tail had been broken at one point, so that the pointed tip was disconnected from the rest, and would probably have hung down limply and trailed on the ground if he tried to walk. His ill-belted stomach had broken through the red cloth of his midriff, his horsehair beard was askew, and beads of sweat had carried streaks of pigment from the widow's peak ineptly painted on his forehead through the barricades of the furry eyebrows that served him instead of a mask, to stain his eyelids brown. It was difficult to estimate his exact age, but he was definitely not young, and I judged that he was probably in his sixties—perhaps too old for the extravagances of the Carnival.

"Are you injured, Signor?" I asked him, anxiously in Italian.

His eyes, which had been closed, opened then and he stared at me dazedly, unblinking in the candlelight.

"Have you been attacked?" I added.

It seemed that he tried to muster a smile. "Not recently," he replied—in English.

Obviously, my accent had given my origin away. His, by contrast, did not. He might conceivably have been a native English-speaker of some sort, but I suspected that he was merely a fluent linguist.

"Are you hurt, then?" I asked, in English, in quest of more specific information.

He met my gaze more directly and more consciously, and seemed to weigh me up. "I'm thirsty," he said, in a faint voice, seemingly absentmindedly—or, at least, not in answer to the question I had posed.

I reached into another pocket and pulled out what Uncle Jerome would have called a "hip-flask." He had an identical one, which he filled with brandy when the opportunity arose, and which was rarely long delayed in being emptied again.

Mine, however, did not contain *eau-de-vie*—although The Devil seemed to have assumed that it did, for when he took the flask from my hand, clutching it awkwardly between his padded paws, and put it to his lips, the expression of amazement that spread over his black-painted visage was a sight to behold.

He looked at me again, questioningly.

"It's all right," I said. "Drink it all, if you have need of it."

He did, with a relish that seemed sufficient reward for my generosity.

"Where did you find that water?" he asked me, curiously, as he handed the empty flask back to me and struggled into a sitting position. "I had not thought that there was any so pure in the whole of...Venice." There was a curious pause before he voiced the city's name, during which he cast glances to the left and right, at either end of the alleyway, as if trying to work out exactly where he was.

"I filled the flask from a spring on a Tyrolean Hill in the foothills of the Alps," I said. "The local guide my uncle had hired told us that it was a holy spring, brought forth from the rock by some saint or other who used to live in a nearby hermitage hundreds of years before—but you must know as well as I do what such tales are worth. All along the route of the Grand Tour, legends are manufactured by the yard, like cheap cotton cloth, for the edification of the Tourists. Even so, I suppose I must have some residue of superstition lurking in the depths of my consciousness, for it's a full fortnight since I filled the flask, and I've saved the water ever since. Whenever I've felt thirsty, I've always thought that a time might come when I have a more desperate thirst, and I took comfort in still having it in my pocket."

"But you no longer have it now," said the Devil, looking at me slightly askance, with an expression that I could not make out beneath his smeared make-up.

"Your need seemed more urgent than any I'm likely to encounter in the near future," I told him.

"Even so," he said, "it was uncommonly kind of you to sacrifice it… for me."

"It seems to have revived you somewhat," I said, "for which I'm glad. I was worried for a moment, when I feared that you might be mortally hurt."

"I've had the same fear myself, on occasion," he replied, inspecting his arms and legs with his eyes, and then flexing them, as if to check them for wounds, "but it has always proven premature."

He looked up and down the street again, then, as if he were still wondering, if not where he was, at least how he came to be there. He shifted his position, and moved his bedraggled tail sideways so that he could sit squarely on a doorstep. The door in question seemed to me to have been condemned long ago and the house to which it belonged was dark and silent.

I made as if to move on, but he reached out with his left hand to grasp my right wrist, and contrived to do it in spite of the awkward finger-squeezing glove.

"Sit down with me for a minute, Signor, if you will," he said.

The clocks had only just chimed eleven, and I was sure that I could find San Giacomo dell'Orio in a matter of minutes, if I stuck to my decision that I actually wanted to be there at midnight, so I sat down willingly enough. I placed the candle-stub on the ground in front of us, so that it illuminated both our faces from below in a strangely eerie fashion.

Those faces would have seemed a strange pair had any other observer been present, my companion's covered in black stickiness and mine shielded by white porcelain. His hair was black and smooth, mine blond and wavy. My eyes were a paler blue then than they are now, while his were very difficult to make out, the irises so dark that his pupils, dilated any case because of the poor light, seemed unnaturally large, giving his stare an ominous quality.

"A feeble imitation of Hellfire, alas, Signor," I said, whimsically, my negligent hand indicating the candle. "I hope you don't find the tiny flame too cool."

"Not at all," he said. Then, after a slight pause, he said: "You know who I am, then?"

"I know who you appear to be," I answered.

"Appearances can be deceptive," he admitted.

"They can," I confirmed. "I have been sometimes been mistaken for an angel myself, it seems, although the people accusing me of it do not always look at me as one might expect them to look at an angel."

"You have fanciful artists to blame for that," the Devil said. "In fact, there are no blond angels, and you do not resemble one at all—but the human imagination has long lost accurate sight of my kind."

"Well, I dare say that you would know the truth of the matter far better than I would," I said. "I was christened Gabriel, which only encourages witty allusions." I offered him my hand and added "Gabriel Bowlands, of Bristol."

He hesitated for a moment, and then took the hand in his fake paw. His grip, although awkward, was firm, and seemingly frank. "I was never christened," he admitted, "but I prefer the name Lucifer to many others."

I laughed. "In your place," I said, "so would I. Bringer of Light is a more flattering cognomen than many that have been applied to you. How is the work of temptation and chastisement going? It must keep you very busy nowadays, I dare say."

"By all means dare," he replied, perhaps a trifle sullenly, and more than a trifle bitterly.

"If it's not impertinent of me to say so," I observed, "you don't seem to be relishing your role at present."

"Would you," he said, "if you were me?" He looked at me askance again, but sounded as if he were genuinely curious to hear my answer.

"No," I admitted, thinking on my feet. "I expect that I might be able to take some enjoyment from the artful aspects of temptation, but I don't believe that I could take any pleasure in punishing sinners, or any pride in such labor."

"Pride?" the Devil queried.

"If I had been cast out of Paradise for such a sin, as legend says of you," I said, meditatively, "I think that I would resent being commanded to punish sinners—it would seem to me to be adding insult to injury."

"You don't think that sinners ought to be punished?" the Devil asked.

"Some surely do," I admitted, "but it has always seemed to me that many in Dante's *Inferno*, let alone his *Purgatorio*, might have been granted forgiveness, and certainly deserved more sympathetic under-standing...the lustful and the slothful as well as the proud."

"You don't consider pride a serious offense against God, then?" he queried.

"Quite frankly, it doesn't seem to me to be a very heinous sin, even when it really does constitute a sin. In fact, I tend to regard pride as a virtue rather than a crime, in most circumstances...and if I were a proud man, and found myself damned in consequence, I would probably think myself direly ill-treated."

He ventured a small laugh himself. "You're a *philosophe*, I pre-sume?" he said, evidently deliberate in refraining from using the equiv-alent English term.

"I'd like to think so," I told him. "And if it's your covert influence that has made me one, I thank you for it, even if it means that I shall never present myself at the Portals of Paradise, soliciting admission."

Abruptly, he sat up straighter, as if he had suddenly remembered something that had been hovering just beyond the grasp of his memory. Again he cast that double glance at either extremity of the dark alley-way, but this time he seemed to have recovered his bearings.

"We're in Venice," he said.

"Indeed we are," I confirmed. "Within a stone's throw of San Gia-como dell'Orio, on the Saturday before Shrove Tuesday."

"And the Portals of Paradise are here." He put his gloved hand to his face then, almost as if he were trying to determine his identity, or the disguise of his flesh. The fake claws came away stained black, and he wiped them on his thigh.

"Well, I wouldn't go that far," I said. "On the other hand, I couldn't find them in Paris, in spite of its reputation, and I had no sooner arrived here that I received an invitation to an amorous assignation, so...who knows?"

He remarkable eyes were looking at me in what seemed to me to be an exceedingly strange manner. "I've recovered my bearings now," he said, in a tone that I could not fathom at all. "I'm greatly in your debt, Master Gabriel."

"Not really," I said. "It was only a drink of water."

"By no means trivial in Venice," he told me, accurately enough, given the difficulty of finding pure water in the city. "And the intention, too, was pure kindness."

I shrugged my shoulders, "That's not so rare," I told him.

He didn't contradict me, but I got the strong impression that he thought the opposite.

"But you have no need of the Portals of Paradise," he said, looking into my eyes.

I tried to laugh, improvising comedy. "To answer that would take me into deep theological waters, where I've never ventured before," I said. "I might need time to ruminate the question."

"I'm sorry," he said. "I misunderstood your reference. You were speaking poetically, not literally. You're a poet as well as a *philosophe*, then?"

"Of course," I said. "Not a versifier, but I hope one day to be a dramatist. I hope to study the particular artistry of Goldoni and Gozzi while I'm here."

"The Commedia?" he said, as if he were still trying to weigh me up, to measure me scrupulously.

"Indeed," I said. "And although Boccaccio called Dante's *Comedia* the *divine* comedy, it has always seemed to me that the *commedia dell'arte* has even more divinity within it, even though it remains earthbound, even in Gozzi's magical fantasies."

The Devil seemed to take that witty remark more seriously than I had intended it, to such an extent that I began to wonder how seriously I *had* intended it.

"So you haven't come to buy the Portals of Paradise," he said. "You're not a man of commerce?"

"Only in the sense that I might one day inherit a firm of cotton merchants," I told him, "and then slightly reluctantly. As a student poet and playmaker, my sin, like yours, if your reputation can be trusted, is pride rather than avarice. I'm content to leave trading tickets to the Portals of Paradise to the costumed hawkers of the Church."

The Devil nodded his head slowly. "I rather like to think of myself as a poet and playmaker too," he said. "I won't say that we have a lot in common, because it might be reckoned an insult, but I'm glad to meet you, and to feel sympathy for you. I shall take a veritable pleasure in redeeming my debt. You're a young man, evidently; are you in love?"

It was a bizarre question for a stranger to ask, even one who seemed to be intent on adopting an avuncular attitude, but there was no point in taking offense. "Only at a distance," I told him, with a brief apologetic laugh. "I have seen the woman of my dreams, but have not had the privilege of speaking to her."

"That I can contrive," he said. "My permission to work miracles is severely restricted, but over matters of amorous passion, I have considerable influence."

"Party of the standard apparatus of temptation, no doubt," I said, finding it very easy to go along with the joke, and enjoyable. "It's a pity, though, that you can't guarantee me success in my theatrical career. For that I might be more willing to trade my soul."

"Don't say that, Signor Gabriel," he said. "This is not vulgar commerce, but a reciprocal gesture of kindness. I cannot guarantee you success in the theatrical world, alas, but I might be able to assist you in your research. Did your studies in Paris introduce you, by any chance, to a drama called *Le Roi en jaune*?"

I laughed. If ever was a play with which the Devil ought to be familiar, I thought, it was that one.

"I've heard the title quoted," I told him, "in English as well as French, but I was under the impression that it's merely a kind of theatrical legend, not a play that actually exists. It's said to be capable of driving men mad, I believe, and features a masked ball at which the Devil appears in person. If it were produced here, of course, it would be largely improvised, so the difficulty of discovering an authentic script would not arise."

"True," said the Devil. "Would you like to see such an…improvisation?"

"I certainly would," I told him, "but there's no mention of it in any of the playbills I've consulted, and I believe that I've researched as many of the theaters of Venice as any mere mortal could in a single day."

"You won't find any indication of the time or place by that means," he told me. "Nor will it be advertised, if it is being advertised at all, as *Il Re giallo*. But it will be performed in the city on the final day of the festival, before Lent begins. If you wish, I can tell you when and where. I can even reserve you a seat in a box."

"Really?" I said.

"I am in your debt," he said, again.

"But we have made no pact?" I observed, stringing out the joke.

"Indeed not," he said. "I have no claim on your soul at all. I am merely… returning a kindness. It is not my reputation, as you know, but you seem convinced that I'm not as black as I'm sometimes painted, and I'm also grateful for that consideration."

As he concluded the last sentence he gripped the glove covering his right hand with his teeth and pulled it off. Then he raised the hand to his theatrical make-up again, and wiped a smear from his cheek with the tip of his index finger…but the greasepaint was applied so thickly that no contrasting skin tone emerged as a result of the operation.

"If you really are the Devil" I said, "perhaps I ought to suspect you of temptation, and the intention of luring me into some kind of trap?"

"Perhaps you ought," he said, mildly, "but even if that were the case, could you resist the temptation in question?"

I laughed. "Certainly not," I said. "It's too perfectly calculated."

"Do you have a piece of paper and something with which to write?" he asked.

I took out the notebook in which I had recorded the details I had taken from miscellaneous theater posters, and presented him with a blank page and a graphite stick carefully wrapped in Bowlands cotton—in those days, not all pencils were encased in wood.

He wrote a set of directions in English, commenting as he did so: "This will enable you to find the street. It's in Dorsoduro, on Guidecca. Once there, you'll find the Teatro Festim easily enough. The performance will begin three hours before midnight on Tuesday" He continued writing, and added: "Show this inscription at the door, and you'll be admitted, and taken to the box. Go alone."

I took the notebook back and looked at the second part of the inscription, which was not in English or Italian, nor in Greek, although the lettering looked more akin to Greek than the Latin alphabet or any of its modern derivatives. I did not query the instruction, though.

"Will you be there?" I asked.

"Most certainly," he said, "although you might not recognize me without this horrid greasepaint. I'll meet you in the box, if I can, although I shall be discreet, and might not arrive until the curtain is about to go up. My presence will undoubtedly be known to certain members of the audience, but I would rather they did not attempt to confront me until the dramatically appropriate moment. Nor would I want any kind of altercation to deflect attention from the comedy, let alone spoil it. I give you my word, for what it may be worth, that your soul will not be in peril, and that although traps will certainly be set by some of those present, you will not come to any harm."

"Should I come as I am?" I asked. Although I was masked, as etiquette required, I was not wearing costume, although my soft English jacket, jerkin and trousers, all in black, were sufficiently distinct from conventional local dress almost to qualify as one. I had not wanted to wear formal dress, with a plastron and cravat, in imitation of the London gentry, but something far more casual—as surely befit an honest

Bristolian—and I dare say that I could have passed, in the context of the Commedia tradition, for one of the less colorful *zanni*.

"That would probably be acceptable," he assured me, after an appraising glance, "but I might be able to find you something more appropriate."

"Not Pantalone, I hope," I quipped.

"Nothing from the Commedia," he assured me. "There will probably be Arlecchinos and Scaramuccias in abundance, and it certainly would not be wise to appear as Il Capitano."

I closed the notebook, and put it back in my pocket. "Thank you," I said, not knowing what else to say. The situation appeared to be so bizarre that there was nothing I could say—but it seemed to me to be the first aspect of the Carnival of Venice I had encountered that day that was not tired and false. No matter how weary the man in the Devil costume had seemed before my draught of water had revived him, and no matter how awkwardly fake his frayed costume and smeared make-up might be, there was an authentic bizarrerie and mystery about his person and his conduct.

To say that I was intrigued by him would have been a drastic understatement. The adventure he was offering me was, indeed, a custom-designed temptation, far more calculated to appeal to my nature than his eccentric offer to assist in my distant courtship, or the amorous note that might or might not have been set by the woman in back who might or might not have been staring at me from her balcony—although, it occurred to me even then that, had I not received the mysterious note handed in at the hotel, I would never have been in that mysterious backstreet, and I would never have stumbled over the exhausted Devil.

I stood up. "I must try to get my bearings," I said. "I ought to be in the square before San Giacomo dell'Orio before midnight, whatever I decide to do thereafter. It was a pleasure to meet you, Signor…Lucifer."

"One word of warning, Signor Gabriel," he said. "No matter how much the play amuses you, you must be careful to stay in the box. I am trying to discharge a debt, not to punish you. If I thought you had any interest in the Portals of Paradise beyond the poetic, I would not have told you where and when *Il Re giallo* is being performed, for fear that you might be one of those it sometimes reduces to insanity. Resist any temptation to develop such an interest, if any such lure is presented to you in the interim. You have sight—try to have foresight as well."

"As a *philosophe*," I told him, "I am confident of my sanity, and I have my own ideas about the Portals of Paradise. I do not covet those offered by any legend or the mythology of any Church."

"Well spoken, my friend," said the Devil. "I envy you your presence of mind. Until Tuesday, then."

"Until Tuesday," I said, bowing politely, even though he did not get up from the doorstep where he was sitting, or offer me any formal gesture of farewell.

V

THE DARK LADY SPEAKS

As the twelfth stroke of midnight sounded in the campanile of San Giacomo dell'Orio, I was pacing back and forth in front of the church, not knowing whether to hope that the man who was supposed to come to meet me would show up or not. I had tried telling myself that the note was just a joke, that it was almost certainly a prank devised by Uncle Jerome to tease and test me, and that either he would appear himself, concealed behind his *bauta*, or perhaps a different mask in order to confuse me, or that no one would appear, and he would wait until I returned to the hotel, crestfallen, in order to laugh at my credulity and confusion.

When the *medico della peste* approached me, therefore, I was half-convinced that it must be my uncle, and even when the man in the mask hissed: "Follow me, Signor Gabriel," in a strong Venetian accent, I was far from sure that he was not simply disguising his voice. In his black hat and long black cloak, he could have been anyone.

Even when he led me to the shore of the lagoon, where a boat was waiting—a large boat with a mast and a sail, not a gondola—I was still uncertain as to whether it was my uncle or not, and it was not until I saw his hands, holding out a sheet of black silk for my inspection, that I became convinced that it was not.

"Must blind your eyes," the Venetian said, seemingly showing the limited scope of his English.

"You want me to wear a blindfold?" I queried, to make absolutely certain that he did not mean what he had said literally.

"Black over eyes," he said. "Secret. Will bring you back same way."

The script seemed perfectly recognizable—practically a cliché: the handsome young man taken to the amorous rendezvous in a blindfold, to meet the mysterious lady. At the time, it was more Drury Lane that the Boulevard du Temple, which had not yet acquired the reputation for theaters specializing in tawdry melodrama that it rapidly acquired during the Empire and the Restoration, but it was recognizable nevertheless.

"Go ahead," I said, figuring that if anyone did mean me harm, they could do it just as easily with my eyes uncovered, given that I had not taken Uncle Jerome's advice and added a rapier to my costume, even though I had one in my luggage.

The blindfold was wrapped around my *volto* and knotted behind my head; because I was masked already it was not unduly uncomfortable. I took my place in the vessel, and it moved away from the quay. I did not make any intensive attempt to deduce where we might be going from incidental sounds, but simply tried to relax into my role. I knew, though, that we certainly made no attempt to navigate a path through the Grand Canal, which was still crowded even at midnight, and I suspected, given the initial impetus of the vessel, that we had headed eastwards from our starting point in Santa Croce and then steered to starboard.

After that, the voyage seemed to last for a long time, and the sounds of the city faded away completely. I deduced that we were almost certainly bound for Murano. When I was eventually helped out of the ship on to dry land again, it was difficult to be sure exactly which way I was heading, but my suspicion was that it was northwards, and that we were probably on San Pietro Martire.

The building that we eventually entered, and whose staircase we climbed, while I was still blindfolded, might conceivably have been a tall building, but we certainly did not go up a sufficient number of stairs to reach an apartment higher than the first floor.

When the blindfold was eventually taken off, I found myself in a room whose windows were heavily curtained as well as shuttered. The hangings on the walls were dark blue and purple, and the illumination provided by a single lamp set on a table was low level, but it displayed quite clearly a sofa on which a woman clad in black, wearing a *moretta muti* and black gloves, was half-lying, and an armchair facing it, separated from it by a small low-topped table on which there were two glasses and an open bottle of red wine.

The woman has the same stature as the woman I had seen from the balcony, and she had similar black hair, but for some reason I could not quite fathom, I suspected from the very start that she was not the woman who had blown me a kiss. Perhaps it was her attitude, or perhaps some kind of instinctive reaction, but something about her made me wary.

As the door closed behind me, the black-clad woman reached out with a hand that seemed remarkably pale, and poured two glasses of wine, even though we were both masked in such a fashion as to have considerable difficulty drinking.

"Please sit down, Mr. Bowlands," said a musical voice, in fluent English, but with a Venetian accent. "Thank you for coming."

"How could I resist such a charming invitation?" I asked, only a trifle sarcastically.

"I was sure that it would appeal to your sense of theatricality," she said, raising her glass. I picked up mine and responded to the evident invitation to clink the two, although she put her glass down again thereafter, and I did likewise. I tried to deduce her age, in spite of the poor lighting and the fact that she was so completely covered, but could not. She had small feet, and slender legs clad in black silk, but there was no clear indication as to whether she was young or old.

"I am going to be very impolite," she said, "and for that I apologize, but I have seen your face before, as I you must suspect, so I hope you will not mind if I ask you to take off your mask."

"Are you going to take yours off, Signora?" I countered.

She did not correct the form of address, as she might have done if I ought to have said Signorina. "No," she said, unsurprisingly—hence no doubt, the admission of impoliteness.

I shrugged my shoulders, and removed the *volto*.

"Now you can drink," she pointed out.

"But it would be impolite for me to do so, since you cannot," I parried.

By way of response, she opened a slit in the fabric or her mask, level with the mouth, and took a sip from her glass. I tried hard to inspect the commissures of her lips for wrinkles, but I could not detect any, nor could I make any judgment based on the lips themselves.

I took a sip from my own glass while attempting an appraisal.

Once again, I was overtaken by a strong impression of being inspected, intently and with focused concentration—but I was not convinced that she was the woman on the balcony.

"Perfect," she said, finally, with a slight hint of regret.

"For what?" I asked.

"For an image of innocence," she told me.

"Are you in need of an image of innocence, then?" I asked. "Am I to be invited to pose as angel for a painter or a sculptor?"

"I would, indeed, like you to pose, if you would be so kind," she said, "but not for a painting or a sculpture."

"As an actor, then?"

"In a manner of speaking. What I would like you to do, if you are agreeable, is to deliver a message."

"Is that all?" I asked, with a deliberate hint of provocation in my voice.

She hesitated, but eventuality said: "For the moment."

Perhaps, I thought, the possibility of an amorous reward was to be held in suspension.

"You seem to have gone to a great deal of trouble merely to summon a messenger," I observed.

"Some messengers," she observed, "are more difficult to summon than others." I had the strong impression that she making an oblique reference to angels, and construed it as a joke, of the kind I had been exchanging with the man costumed as the Devil not long before.

"I dare say that my divine duties will not forbid me to accept an earthly commission," I remarked. "To whom must I take your message, if I consent to be its bearer?"

Instead of answering that question, she said: "It is a message I dare not attempt to deliver myself, nor can I have it delivered by any of my servants, as I had my invitation to you delivered. It is a…delicate matter."

"Evidently," I said. "But why me, of all the people in Venice—someone you have only glimpsed on the balcony of a hotel for a matter of seconds?"

I was obviously fishing for information, but she did not seem resentful. "I saw you in Paris," she said. "I knew that you were coming to Venice for the Carnival. I was slightly anxious when you were late arriving. I know a little about you, and I believe that I can trust you. More importantly, the person to whom I wish to send the message will trust you."

"Why?" I asked. "Has he seen me in Venice too?"

She made a slight sound that might have been a strangled laugh. "No," she said, "but he will read your hand, and he is something of a magician. He will know that you are honest."

"Really?" I said. "And it's purely for my evident honesty that you summoned me? My uncle will be direly disappointed—he's convinced that your interest in me was a matter of lust at first sight, and that you bid me come here in order to make mad, passionate amour."

She continued to study me for a moment. At the present range, even in the dim light, I could see something of the eyes behind the mask. They were dark brown, with silky lashes. The skin surrounding them seemed smooth, without overmuch wrinkling, but I was still reluctant to conclude that she was as young as her silky black hair seemed to imply. The strong impression I had, although I could not have listed a single item of hard evidence, was that she was older than me, and perhaps considerably older.

"Your uncle will be disappointed?" she queried, eventually. "But not you?"

"I can hardly measure the possible extent of my own disappointment while you insist on keeping the mask on," I countered.

"It would be dangerous to take it off," she told me. To judge by the tone of her voice, she regretted that, but exactly why I could not divine.

"For you or for me?"

"For me," she said. "It is perhaps unlikely that you would remember having seen me in Paris, or be able to put a name to my face if you did, but even so, there are powerful reasons for me to maintain my incognito completely."

"According to my uncle," I hazarded, "the resident of the apartment opposite our hotel room is the widow of Giacomo Senedese."

"I can understand the process of his inference," she countered, "but the identification is incorrect."

Given that the widow Senedese was highly unlikely to have been in Paris the previous Autumn, I believed her. "And in what danger would delivering your message place me?" I asked.

"None, if you follow my instructions precisely," she said.

"Than why did your note ask whether I was brave?"

"It's possible that you might find the circumstances of the delivery a trifle intimidating," she said, "but there really is no need to be afraid; the intended recipient will welcome the information, and the guild of *bravi* will not harm an innocent messenger."

At this point, I ought to digress in order to explain her reference, although you have doubtless heard the word "bravo" before and have probably recognized its plural. In Venice, as in many other cities, there has long been a guild for every craft, and every guild claims great antiquity and total control over its trade. Each has its own livery, which is worn with pride—and so deeply entrenched is the system in the Republic that even robbers and assassins dared to form a guild three hundred years ago, and adopted a uniform of their own. They were the *bravi*: killers for hire. Because all guildsmen are sworn to defend and avenge one another, it became exceedingly difficult in the heyday of the *bravi* for any agent of the law to take action against any individual *bravo* without placing himself in extraordinary danger.

The Republic even passed a law at one point in time guaranteeing a free pardon to any bravo who assassinated another, but the ruse failed, and sterner measures had to be taken. In theory, the *bravi* had been suppressed by the end of the seventeenth century, but in fact they never died out, no matter how fiercely they were persecuted and punished, and even in the 1780s, rumor still persisted of a thriving underground organization. Although the old uniform of the *bravi* was by then a carnival costume like any other, at least some pretended *bravi* were probably *bravi* in truth, and the cleverest were reputed to be a veritable personification of danger, violence and treachery.

If the guild of *bravi* was involved in the "delicate matter" in regard to which the dark lady wanted me to deliver a message, then I could understand why she might feel the need to appoint a messenger who was not Venetian.

"There is a question of vendetta in this affair then?" I suggested, to let her know that no matter how innocent I might be, I was not a fool.

"Yes," she agreed. "But that concerns me, and the man to whom the message must be delivered. An innocent messenger will not be running any risk."

"But you are? Mortal risk?"

"I cannot deny it," she said. "There are matters of life and death at stake here. Blood might be spilled, but I hope with all my heart to avoid it. That is the whole purpose of what I am doing. The *bravi* never forget or forgive, but the passage of time erodes anger, and I believe as well as hope that the matter can be settled now by treaty."

"And what if I were to refuse to serve as your messenger?"

"I will find someone else. I still have time in hand. You are certainly under no threat from me, my angel."

I did not challenge the epithet. "And what if I accept? Were you thinking of offering a bribe, or simply relying on my chivalrous instincts...or angelic nature?"

"I had hoped and expected that an English gentleman with a spirit of adventure might carry out the commission without making vulgar demands for payment."

"You know my name," I pointed out, "so you presumably know that I'm not an English gentleman in any strict sense, merely the son and grandson of merchants."

"Aspirations are often worth far more than achievements," she replied. "To tell the truth, I would be reluctant to trust an Englishman who was only a gentleman by title. I know a little more about you than your name—perhaps not enough to be certain that I can trust you, but enough to give me the hope."

"How much more do you know?" I asked, curiously.

"I know that you have a strong interest in the theater, and that you are an admirer of the French *philosophes*," she said, with a hint of irony, as if there were something else that she knew but was deliberately not stating. "Is that information secret?"

Obviously, it was not. Five minutes of conversation with Uncle Jerome could have winkled out that much while he was out drinking one evening, or even five minutes spent eavesdropping on his conversation. Uncle Jerome could be voluble even in casual conversation with strangers.

"Will you tell me what the message is and to whom I have to deliver it before I agree to do it?" I asked, still fencing, although I had no particular reason to prevaricate, having already decided that I would definitely follow the adventure through.

She hesitated again, but then said: "Yes, if you swear to me that if you decide not to do it, you will not tell a living soul what I have said to you—you might place me in danger if you were to do so."

"I swear," I said.

She still hesitated, however, before she said: "As you have doubtless observed if you have walked in the city, there are numerous booths set up in and around the Piazza San Marco, selling all kinds of wares and exhibiting various kinds of performers. One of those booths carries a painted sign bearing the image of an old man and a crystal ball, bearing the legend *Mercutio, Cheiromancer*. Its door is guarded by a burly man costumed as Arlecchino. You will have no difficulty gaining access, and when the cheiromancer has inspected the contours and lines of your hand, he will know who you are, so you may deliver the message. Seek other enlightenment from him if you wish."

"And the message I'm to whisper"'

She hesitated yet again, but finally added: "Tell him that the lady would dearly like possession of the Portals of Paradise to be settled by negotiation, and that he has her guarantee of safe conduct if be cares to come to the Teatro Festim on the Eve of Lent."

That sent something like an electric shock through me, and before I could stop myself, I had blurted out: "The Teatro Festim on Guidecca, where *Il Re giallo* is to be performed?"

I regretted making that revelation within a split second, although there was really nothing to regret. I honestly do not know how she reacted to what I had said; however her complexion might have been altered and whatever expression might have shown on her face was completely hidden by the *moretta*. She maintained silence long enough to prevent any emotion showing in her voice.

Finally, though, she said: "Who told you that *Il Re giallo* is to be staged at the Teatro Festim, my angel?"

I decided that it was my turn to play the role of hoarder of mysteries. "Why should I not know?" I asked, trying to maintain my image as a personification of innocence, even without the assistance of a mask. "As you said yourself, I have a strong interest in all the theaters of Venice. I've been seeking information about all of them from every possible source since I arrived."

"But who told you that *Il Re giallo* would be staged at the Festim?" she repeated, her voice measurably colder than before.

"I don't know my informant's real name," I said, speaking slowly while I made my decision, "but he was costumed as the Devil."

Once again, her reaction was fully masked and quite immeasurable. She sat still for a long minute, before saying, in a tone that was no longer steely, although she could not quite contrive to make it as seductive as she probably hoped: "Where did you meet this Devil, Signor Gabriel, and under what circumstances?"

"I stumbled over him in a back-street in Santa Croce while I was on my way to the rendezvous that you had given me," I said. "I stopped because I feared that he might be hurt. I gave him a drink of water, and we conversed for a while. I mentioned my interest in the theater, and he told me about the play. It seems to me, my lady, that you probably have a better chance of deducing his identity than I do."

She took a long sip of wine in order to give herself time to think, before eventually saying, dryly: "Undoubtedly." She did not elaborate, and obviously had no intention of doing so—but her pronunciation of the word was slightly uncertain, as if she had some doubt as to whether the conclusion to which she had immediately jumped was really correct. After a further sip of wine, she refilled her glass, and mine, even though mine was still half-full. Then she said: "Did your Devil mention the Portals of Paradise?"

"Yes, after I had used the phrase first, poetically—but I thought we might have been talking at cross purposes even at the time, and I'm certain of it now. What are the Portals of Paradise that are going to be at the Teatro Festim at midnight, after the supposed performance of *Il Re giallo*?"

"Will you deliver the message?" she asked, instead of answering the question.

"Yes I will," I said. "Why should I not, given that we both seem to have deduced that I have already been used, unwittingly, to deliver a message to you, and was presumably chosen to do so for much the same reason?"

"Thank you," she said. After a pause, she added: "I do not believe that this alters any assurance I have given you. You will not be running any risk."

"Unlike you?" I queried.

She did not offer any confirmation. She was staring at me from behind her mask, I knew. I met her gaze as best I could. I didn't suppose for a moment that she was capable of reading my thoughts, but she might have thought otherwise.

"You're intending to go to the Festim," she said, not giving it the intonation of a question. "You intend to be there on the Eve of Lent."

I shrugged my shoulders, and said: "I wouldn't have missed it for the world, my lady, even if you hadn't invited me to this bizarre tête-à-tête. How many chances does a theater lover have to see *Il Re giallo?*"

"And you have reason to think that you'll be admitted?"

"Yes," I said, simply. "The Devil gave me some kind of pass."

"*Merda!*" she said, softly. "The seal on the letter I sent you wasn't broken, by any chance?"

"No."

"No, of course not—but that doesn't mean that it wasn't read. *Merda*! It was after you received the note, of course, that you met this… person costumed as the Devil?"

"Yes."

She seemed restless now, although she did not get to her feet. She was sitting up, with her dainty feet in the floor, leaning forward, seemingly concentrating hard.

"There is no reason why you should not deliver the message," she muttered, as if to herself. "Indeed, you surely must. But you honestly do not know what the Portals of Paradise are? You have never heard the legend?"

"Not yet," I said. "But I hope that you're going to tell me, my lady."

She paused for thought yet again, but then said: "If you really have been promised admission to the theater, you'll certainly find out then, if not before, and anyone you ask can probably give you a version of the story, but will you allow me to give you some advice, *mon bel ange?*"

"Please do," I said, trying hard not to sound overly ironic.

"Don't go. Don't go to the Teatro Festim on the Eve of Lent."

"And miss the only chance I'll ever have to see a performance of *Il Re giallo?*"

"Precisely. You do know, obviously, that it has the reputation of driving men mad?"

"So it's said."

"But you don't believe it?"

"No."

"Believe me, my angel," she said, "if you go to that performance, you'll see men who are already mad, and others driven mad. I don't say that it will happen to you, but madness there will surely be, no matter how hard I try to prevent it—all the more so now that the Devil in involved."

"But you intend to be there, do you not?"

This time, she did not bother to hesitate, or even to put on a show of hesitation. "Of course," she said, "but I have no alternative."

"And what about Mercutio the Cheiromancer? Will he be in danger, in spite of your guarantee of safe conduct, now that the Devil is involved? Or is he one of those who will be putting others in danger?"

She made a strangled sound that might have been a laugh. "His presence there certainly won't decrease the danger that certain people might be in, if he isn't appeased by my gesture of good faith," she said. "But no, I don't believe that anyone will try to harm him, unless he tries to harm them?"

"You still haven't told me what the Portals of Paradise are," I pointed out.

"I know," she said. "I'm still thinking…about how much I ought to tell you, beyond the mere fact, and whether I ought to ask you for something more than merely delivering the message."

"Thus far," I said, "I've only promised to deliver a message. Any further requests might require further bargaining."

"I'm aware of that," she snapped. She switched to the Italian language then, presumably to address herself without my being able to follow her, even though the first few comments, at least, were apparently addressed to me. I can't be entirely certain that I did follow all of it, but the best estimate I can make of what she said can be translated as: "No, innocent as you my be, how can I possibly trust you now? You have no idea what you're involved with, but you're involved nevertheless. Angel or not, it not worth any further risk. Far too much has been risked and lost already, over decades. I can understand that your curiosity won't allow you to let it go, now—and I have to take the responsibility for piquing it in the first place, but there might be no harm done. Perhaps there won't be a fight, no matter what the outcome of the auction is, if we can even progress to that kind of bargaining. Perhaps, all things considered, it would be best if we didn't…but it's too late to turn back. There are too many people already mad, who can't let go."

For a few moments she had been looking anywhere but at me, while she rambled on, following her train of thought, but now her gaze returned to my angelic face, with sufficient intensity to make my hand twitch as if to replace the *volto* and shield myself. I calmed it, though, and simply said, yet again: "What are the Portals of Paradise, my lady?"

She shrugged her shoulders. "They're two of the eyes that the Devil enabled Pietro Beroviero to make in Murano for Bartolomeo Collatino, nine-and-thirty years ago."

For a moment, I was tempted to think that I was none the wiser, but I was. I knew that when the mystery woman said "eyes" she had to be talking about glass eyes, and if the Devil was supposed to have enabled Pietro Beroviero to make them, they were presumably magical, or supposed so be.

Murano, as I've already mentioned, is the island where the glassmakers of Venice had and still have their workshops. There was a time when Venice was the sole master of all the great secrets of the glassmaking art, and I knew that it would be foolish to think that all those secrets had lost when the alchemist Antonio Neri had published his treasonous *Arte Vetraria* at the beginning of the seventeenth century. As a *philosophe*, naturally, I did not believe that those secrets had included genuinely magical secrets, but I knew that many people did believe it. If a pair of glass eyes existed that were reputed to have magical properties—presumably, at the very least, the power of restoring sight to men who had lost their eyes, and perhaps providing a kind of sight in some way preferable that provided by nature's eyes—they would be something worth haggling over, or bidding to acquire at an auction...and perhaps worth killing in order to obtain them.

According to Uncle Jerome, I remembered, the Giacomo Senedese who had previously owned the apartment opposite our hotel room was the descendant of a family once influential in Murano. That might help to explain how the dark lady, evidently a resident of Murano herself, had obtained access to it in order to pose for me on the balcony...or, more likely, to delegate someone else to pose for me, wearing a costume similar to the one she was presently wearing.

I wanted to prompt further revelations, so I said: "So Beroviero was a glassmaker?" I said. "And doubtless an alchemist too? And Bartolomeo Collatino was...what? A man who had lost his eyes as result of judicial torture in the infamous Piombi?"

I had no reason to think that the gruesome tortures and punishments reputedly still carried out in the infamous Venetian prison included deliberate blinding, but it seemed like a fair guess, in context.

She was staring at me again, but she wasn't fooled into thinking that I'd ever heard of either of the people she'd mentioned. "Something like that," she agreed, her voice having become neutral and controlled again.

"And the glass eyes in question are reputed to produce visions of paradise?"

"Exactly," she confirmed, although I wasn't sure what the exactitude was supposed to signify.

"A valuable property, then—if, as you say, the ones that are to be auctioned on Tuesday are authentic."

"Very," she agreed. "It's said that there are people who would be willing to put out their own eyes in order to make the substitution, if, as you say, they could be persuaded that they had the genuine article in their possession. As for men already blind, who could put them to the test…"

"They'd be doubly keen to acquire them," I concluded, but added: "And they might be useful partners in a confidence trick…and dangerous allies."

"You're a quick thinker, my angel," she observed, in a dry tone suggestive of something more than a mere compliment.

"But not the kind of man to put out his eyes, even if he could be convinced that he had a pair of magical substitutes to hand," I assured her. "How about you?"

"I'm too fond of my own eyes to consider such a possibility," she replied, "but mere possession of the eyes is supposed to grant considerable visionary gifts. If anyone could contrive to reunite them after all this time…but thus far no one has, and not for want of trying."

"And not only on your part, I assume?"

"By no means," she told me.

"And the man costumed as the Devil is another interested party, obviously?"

"Obviously," she echoed. "If you happen to see him again before the Eve of Lent, my angel, would you do me the favor of telling him what I've asked you to tell Mercutio, and that it also applies to him, with all my heart?"

I had said that further requests might require further bargaining, but that had only been making conversation, and I thought I now had evidence enough that she was not a young woman at all, and that any amorous favors granted might be more precious to her than to me. "Yes, I'll do that," I said. "Do you think he'll accept?"

"He might," she said. "He took the trouble to intercept you, and give me warning of his intention…but whether that means that he's willing to let bygones be bygones, I really don't know. The Devil, like the *bravi*, is reputed never to forget or forgive."

"But who is he, really?" I asked.

"I can't be absolutely sure. You don't believe, then, that he's really the Devil?"

I laughed "No, I don't—and nor do you, it seems. But all the time I was talking to him, we were both pretending that he really was the Devil, as a kind of running joke. At least, I thought it was a joke, on his part as well as mine. It's sometimes said, though, that the Devil's greatest asset is the ability to persuade us that he doesn't exist. He took care to tell me at one point that appearances are deceptive, implying that he meant that his appearance as the Devil was deceptive…but perhaps he meant that his appearance as a blatantly counterfeit Devil was deceptive. As a *philosophe*, though, I can't take the possibility that he's genuine seriously…and more than I can take seriously the notion of a pair of glass eyes that give their possessor the ability to see Paradise."

"That lack of imagination might be a precious asset, my angel. Be careful you don't lose it on the Eve of Lent."

I couldn't help resenting the accusation that I lacked imagination. I was a playmaker, after all, and one who appreciated Carlo Gozzi. What I lacked was the capacity to believe in the artifacts of comedy. On the other hand, if she was correct to say that men existed who were mad enough to pluck out their own eyes in pursuit of the dream of a pair of glass eyes that might enable them to obtain visions of paradise, then a lack of imagination would certainly be an asset in that circumstance. And I knew full well that there were hundreds of thousands of people mad enough to believe in the Devil, and at least a few mad enough to believe that they might be the Devil. Perhaps the person who had tripped me up in the back-street had been more sincere that I had assumed—and if my dark lady really did believe in the Portals of Paradise, and their diabolical origin, it might only have required a simple logical extrapolation for her to conclude that I really had brought her a message from the Devil.

Whatever the truth of the matter, that message had obviously complicated her plans considerably. From my point of view, as a spectator, the comedy was becoming increasingly intriguing.

"Tell me more about Pietro Beroviero and Bartolomeo Collatino, my lady," I requested, politely, thinking that I needed to fill in the backstory if I was fully to appreciate the comedy as it played out.

"You don't need me to tell you that," she said, dismissively. "Ask the cheiromancer—he's said to tell the tale quite well, and knows even more than he usually tells. He won't refuse…but even if he did, any bear-leader who's brought Tourists to Venice before should know it— your uncle probably heard it a generation ago, although he's likely forgotten it in the interim."

I made a mental note to ask him, before or after I solicited the tale from Mercutio the Cheiromancer.

"At midnight on Tuesday, when Lent officially begins," I ventured, "custom presumably requires that everyone will take off their masks... including everyone at the performance of *Il Re giallo* at the Teatro Festim?"

This time, the sound she strangled was definitely a laugh. "Custom would usually require that," she agreed. "But the custom might lack force, in the circumstances...especially if madness prevails."

"So I shall see your face then?"

"It's possible. But will you recognize me when—or if—my mask comes off? I doubt that I'll be the only woman there."

"So you're still adamant that you won't unmask for me now?"

"Absolutely."

"And there's nothing I could offer to do for you for which you might be willing to trade that favor?"

"No."

"Uncle Jerome will be dreadfully disappointed."

"Don't tell him. Tell him that we spent all the time since midnight doing whatever you please. That would, at any rate, might be wiser than telling him that the Devil has obtained you an entry to a play that reputedly drives men mad, and an auction at which the Portals of Paradise will be sold to the highest bidder, if violence doesn't prevent the sale from taking place. If you do that, he might conclude that you're already mad."

She had a point.

She reached for a hand-bell that was on the table where the lamp was set, and shook it. "You'll be taken back to the shore where you boarded the boat now," she said. "I'm sorry if the journey has been a disappointment."

"Well," I said, "I have no cause for complaint. Your note only promised me an adventure, and you've certainly offered me that, with a little help from the Devil." I raised my glass, in a mock salute. "Whatever happens henceforth, you have my gratitude."

"Thank you, my angel," she said, blandly, as the door opened behind me and the man in the *medico della peste* reappeared. "And in anticipation, you have mine."

I replaced my *volto*, and meekly allowed the silk scarf to be knotted over the eye-holes. Then the servant led me away, down the stairs, through various corridors, across paving stones, and back to the boat. The surroundings were absolutely silent.

As we neared the Venetian shore on the way back, I heard several bells chime four o'clock, almost simultaneously, but I hadn't been in Venice long enough to be able to recognize any of the carillons. I was put ashore in Santa Croce, though, after presumably doubling the western extremity of the island group, and the dark lady's servant gave me an ironic bow before leaping back aboard the ship, which veered away instantly.

By the time I got back to the hotel, Uncle Jerome was fast asleep, but I knew that the inquisition had only been postponed.

VI

THE BLIND CHEIROMANCER

The Saturday on which I had met the Devil was the seventeenth of February, and the Sunday in the early hours of which I had my rendezvous with the dark lady—Motherbank Sunday in some reckonings—was the eighteenth, but it was not cold in Venice by the standards of English winters; the temperature seemed quite mild to me, and the night not unduly long, even though the equinox was still more than a month away.

Uncle Jerome was not a man to go to any church but an Anglican one, and although the Bowlands were traditionally a high church family, accustomed to imitation Roman Catholic ceremonies, my uncle was a dedicated foe of what many people would have considered the authentic rite. We therefore spent a leisurely morning eating a lengthy breakfast.

"I was worried last night when you didn't come back," he confessed. "I expected to see you, briefly at least, before you went to your rendezvous—indeed, I wasn't at all sure that you had any such intention."

"I had to go," I assured him, "if only to discover whether it was all a trick on your part. I was quite surprised to find that it wasn't."

"It was serious, then? It really was an amorous assignation? Was it the Senedese widow?"

"It did seem to be an amorous assignation of sorts," I said, "but it was far less exciting than you might imagine. We talked a good deal, and drank a little wine. The lady didn't remove her mask, let alone her clothes. I have no idea who she is, or exactly where the rendezvous took place, although it was somewhere in Murano, and I now have reason to suspect that she's a good sixty years old."

"Ah!" said Uncle Jerome, in what he probably intended to be to a neutral tone. "But she didn't make any attempt to seduce you?"

"None—nor did I make any attempt to make love to her. Perhaps that was yet another opportunity allowed to lapse, because I was insufficiently bold?"

"That doesn't explain why she didn't try to make love to you," Uncle Jerome observed.

"True," I agreed. "Perhaps I proved to be disappointing, seen at closer range—not a true angel after all."

"You're telling me that nothing happened at all? Really? That she took you all the way to Murano all for nothing?" He seemed skeptical. He thought—probably hoped—that I was simply being diplomatic. I couldn't blame him. He was right, after all, except in his estimate of what it was that I was discreetly concealing from him.

"She claimed to have seen me in Paris," I said, "and she seemed to know quite a lot about me. She called me *my angel* continually, but so many middle-aged woman saw me in Paris and used similar expressions. I can't remember any Venetians, though—can you?"

"No, but if there were any Venetians lurking about, Kenavan will know. I'll ask him."

"Do," I said. "By the way, do the names Pietro Beroviero and Bartolomeo Collatino mean anything to you?"

"No. Should they?"

"Apparently, there's some local legend attached to them, which is routinely recited to Tourists, and probably was twenty-some years ago."

"I don't remember."

"The legend apparently concerns a pair of glass eyes known as the Portals of Paradise."

Uncle Jerome furrowed his brow, but shook his head. "Means nothing to me," he said. "Kenavan will know. I'll ask him about that too."

"What a useful fount of wisdom he is," I observed, dryly.

"I don't know why you don't like the fellow," Uncle Jerome said. "He seems pleasant enough to me—and as you say, he's a real fount of wisdom."

"If he does know my lady from Murano," I said, thoughtfully, "perhaps it's from him that she heard about me. She mentioned that she's been looking forward to my arrival—and you said that Kenavan was asking about me too."

Uncle Jerome shrugged. "Does it matter that your mystery woman knows something about you, or where she got the information from if she did?"

"Probably not," I admitted. "I don't have any secrets, do I? Except for secrets from you, Uncle, obviously."

"What secrets?" he enquired.

"If I told you, they wouldn't be secrets, would they?"

He shook his head dismissively. "I picked up some information myself last night," he told me. "The Harringtons are definitely here, and I know where they're staying. If the girl runs true to form, though, you'll probably run into her anyway if you're going to go to the theater every night. Are you going to try and talk to her if you do, in spite of the dragon lady?"

"Perhaps," I said.

"You should," he recommended. Then curiosity got the better of him. "Are you going to see your mystery woman again, then?"

"I don't know," I said. "Will I recognize her if I do? If she changes her mask…Venice can be a very confusing place at this time of year."

"True—and if she really is sixty… Anyway, are we going to complete the tour that we began yesterday, and had to cut short?"

"Actually," I said, "I think I'm ready to begin exploring on my own."

"On your own?" he said suspiciously.

"Yes."

His face brightened. "You don't, by any chance, have another assignation?" Then his face fell again. "Or are you just thinking of going to prowl around the Harringtons? Maybe I shouldn't even tell you where they're staying."

"I'm not," I assured him, "so you needn't. Even if, as you say, Adelaide goes to the theater, there's only a slim chance that we might be present at the same performance, and if we're both masked…well it really doesn't seem to be worth worrying about. Thank you for enquiring, though."

"Do you want me to make further enquiries about the widow Senedes?"

"No, that's all right" I said. "And on second thoughts, don't bother to ask Kenevan about Venetian ladies in Paris or the two names I mentioned to you, if you run into him. It's not worth the trouble."

I had my own ideas, of course, about how to follow up the indications provided by the two names in question.

"I suppose you'll be going to the theater again tonight, even though it's Sunday," he said, with a sigh.

"Of course," I said. "We're not in Bristol now. It's the Carnival of Venice, and the Carnival of Venice knows no day of rest. Everyone will go to Church, and then put on their masks again, and resume their ritual performances of the other kind."

That gave him an idea. "If you went to mass at San Giacomo dell'Orio, you might get an opportunity to see the widow Senedes without her moretta," he said.

"But doubtless wearing mourning veils," I pointed out. "And what would be the point?"

"True," he conceded. "Well, whatever you're going to do *on your own*, enjoy yourself—and whenever you're ready to complete our little tour, just let me know. I'm supposed to be your guide and mentor, remember."

"I haven't forgotten," I assured him.

When I left the hotel, I set a course for the Piazza. Although, as I had said to Uncle Jerome, the Carnival was non-stop, the streets were noticeable quieter than the day before, with a far greater proportion of people devoid of masks and costumes. The closer I got to San Marco, however, the more the appearance of the Carnival reasserted itself, albeit in a slightly dispirited fashion.

As soon as I set foot in the crowded square, a Pierrot approached me and handed me a piece of paper. That was no longer a cause for surprise, so I barely glanced down at it, expecting to see yet another a crudely-printed playbill advertising a performance later that day. That was exactly what I did see: an advertisement for *Il Diavolo in Bagdad*, a comedy "in the manner of Carlo Gozzi," to be staged that afternoon between three and five o'clock.

The Pierrot was still standing before me, as if expecting a reaction. When I looked back at his white-painted face, he said, in English: "We all hope that you'll be able to come, Signor Bowlands. It's the première."

"Do you know me, then?" I asked him, looking him in his heavily made-up but unmasked face. His slightly bloodshot eyes met my own gaze frankly.

He laughed. "Yes, Signor, and you know me—it's the costume, no doubt, that renders me unrecognizable. You saw me in Paris more than once. Signor Landini asked me to be sure to look out for you, and to give you his regards. He'll be delighted when I tell him that I found you—you will come, won't you?"

"Yes, of course," I said, still struggling to place him—but he was right, as Pierrot, he was unrecognizable. I could not connect him to whatever part he'd played in *Turandot*, or any other performances by the Landini company I had seen. For a moment, I wondered whether he might perhaps have been my devil of the previous evening, but he seemed too young, and too slight in his build. Even with the obscuring effects of white make-up instead of black, I decided, it was definitely not the same face.

"It seems to be a rather short play," I commented, for the sake of saying something.

"It will be exactly as long as it needs to be," he said, "as you will readily appreciate, Signor Bowlands, as a practitioner of the dramatic art yourself."

Given the way that I was dressed, it was not particularly surprising that I was recognizable in spite of my mask, but the discovery of yet another person in Venice who seemed to have been eagerly awaiting my arrival seemed utterly bizarre—although, when I considered the matter, there was nothing particularly surprising in the fact that the Landini troupe had returned home for the Carnival, or that Signor Landini remembered the English Tourist who had questioned him so eagerly about the Venetian theater.

"It's kind of you to classify me thus," I said, still speaking English, "given that I've never actually had a play produced. And I'm surprised that you seem to value my opinion so highly. I might not be able to follow the play very well, you know—my Italian is poorer than my French."

"But you saw us in Paris," Pierrot said, blithely. "You understand our technique. And you saw *Il Mostro turchino* last night, I believe. Our play is in a similar vein."

"How on earth do you know that?" I asked him.

"The world of the Commedia is smaller than you might imagine, my lord," he replied, "and also broader. We had no performance, and several of the company were in the audience. You were seen, and recognized—it's your hair, you see, and the style of your clothing. If you want to travel the city incognito, you'll need a far better disguise."

What he said was plausible enough, and I had not the slightest reason to doubt it, but even so, the encounter was one more link in what seemed to be extending into a chain of coincidences that was beyond the merely remarkable. Had I been more credulous I might almost have begun to believe that I was being devil-led.

"I'll be there, Signor," I said, holding up the playbill, "and thank you for the invitation."

Pierrot bowed, and resumed his slow journey through the crowd, offering his advertisements to possible patrons. I took another look at the playbill, but it was written in Italian, and I had already decided that I would attend the performance in question, so here seemed little point in deciphering it in quest of further information. I folded it up carefully and put it in my pocket. Then I continued on my way across the Piazza, looking from side to side at the stalls and tents pitched there.

Although Sunday did not interrupt the Carnival, the appetite of the crowd in the Piazza for amusement seemed distinctly subdued by comparison with the previous day, and some of the stallholders had not yet opened their establishments, even though it was not long before noon. The jugglers seemed to have put away their clubs and the fire-eaters had extinguished their brands; the celebrations had not stopped, but there was a definite lull in their artificial enthusiasm. I got the impression, though, that the mountebanks had not grown weary of their own deceptions, and that there was not one among them who could not have raised himself for one last effort if required. They were not exhausted, but merely pausing for breath and husbanding their resources, saving themselves for the final assault of the final two days of the festival. There was a curious kind of anticipation in the air, as if everything had slowed down and entered into a phase of suspension, but was still preparing for a final surge.

There was more than one fortune-teller's tent sporting an image of a crystal ball—indeed, there were half a dozen—but I did not have to search for long before spotting the legend advertising Mercutio the Cheiromancer. There was, as predicted, an Arlecchino stationed at the door of the tent, but he was merely standing there, not even putting on a pretence of trying to attract customers.

As I approached, Arlecchino's eyes, visible behind his black mask, fixed themselves upon me, scanned me from top to toe and evaluated me in a trice. Presumably, he did not identify me instantly, as Pierrot had, but he must have seen at a glance that I was an Englishman.

"Would you like to know your future, my lord?" he asked me, in English. His accent was not as strong as Pierrot's, and was not specifically Venetian. It was hoarse, suggesting that it had been working hard enough in recent days to have been strained excessively.

"I believe I would," I said. When I handed him a silver coin he bowed expansively, and lifted the flap that he was guarding.

It was dark inside the tent, all natural light being excluded, but a lantern containing a single candle had been lit, apparently for the convenience of paying customers—except that one side of the lantern-glass was smoked, so that the chair where the cheiromancer sat was shadowed. The chair set before the little table was easy enough to see, but the fortune-teller was merely a vague blur for my unadapted eyes.

It was not until I had taken my place and he leaned forward to take my right hand that I could discern anything definite about him, but in the split second before he lowered his head, clad in a *bauta*, the eyes visible within the holes on the mask—or what he had instead of eyes—caught a ray of light that crept through a gap in the smoke obscuring the lamp-glass.

Perhaps I should not have been surprised to find that he was blind, but no matter how fully prepared I might have been, I would still have felt a shock as I beheld that sightless stare. Even English glass-makers can produce false eyes that simulate the real thing, and the Venetians are so artful that they can make a perfect match to an eye that survives, but Mercutio's false eyes must have been made of jet, for they were as black and glossy as a scarab's carapace.

He had reached out with his left hand and I placed my right hand within it, palm upwards. He began to run the fingertips of his own right hand over mine, very gently. Not content to track the lines inscribed on the palm, and the general contours of the hand he examined my fingers, and even my wrist.

"A gentleman," he murmured, in Italian, "and a man well-used to plying a pen," he said, obviously having taken account of the general condition of my hands and the callus on the joint of my middle finger.

I confirmed those unremarkable deductions, speaking Italian although I knew that my origins would be clear enough.

Like almost everyone else I had addressed in Italian since arriving in Venice he immediately switched to my own language, as easily and fluently as his dubious friend the Devil. "How do you like the carnival, my lord?" he asked, in a voice whose softness and unctuousness seemed blatantly contrived. "It is the experience of a lifetime, is it not? You will remember it fondly when you are eighty years old, I think—all the more so because your children and your children's children will not have the opportunity to see its like."

"Are they fated never to leave home, then?" I asked, ironically.

"No, my lord," he replied. "They will be great travelers—but Venice will not be the same. The Republic will be gone, the city looted by a dwarfish conqueror from the west. There will be carnivals here, as there will be everywhere, but they will not be the Carnival that you have seen. Make the most of your opportunity, my lord—you are a fortunate man to be here this day. You may never be quite as fortunate again, even though you will live long and prosper."

"I'm glad to hear that," I said, agreeably, "and very sorry to learn that the fate of this great city will be worse than mine. Where will you make your living then?"

"There will be no necessity, my lord," he said, in a voice so gentle as to belie the bleakness of the sentiment. "Are there any particular matters you would like me to address, in reading your hand?"

"Yes," I said. "As you have observed, I'm fond of wielding a pen. Can you tell me something about what I might write, and what its fate will be?" I was speaking quietly, even though I had nothing, as yet, to conceal, in case anyone was listening.

"Certainly," he said. "You will labor hard and obstinately, writing lines for others to speak. That work will be your pride and joy. It will bring you esteem, but not a fortune. Gold will come, but from other sources."

My eyes had grown used to the gloom now, and I could make out the shape of his body, if not the color of his robe He was a big man, and broad-shouldered. The hand that held mine was not a laborer's hand, but it was capacious, and strong. It was holding mine very gently, but gave the impression that it could crush it like a vice if it were so inclined, without undue effort.

"You say that I shall have children, and grandchildren?" I asked.

"Yes, my lord. They will give you cause for pride."

"And their mother?"

He hesitated. "You are a wise enough man, my lord," he finally said, "to know that the course of amour rarely runs smooth, but there will be beauty, and there will be joy, and you must make the most of them when and while you can."

"That sounds rather ominous," I remarked.

"No, my lord," he said, a trifle sadly, "merely realistic. No man's life runs entirely smooth, even if he is fated to live long and prosper. Amour is ever treacherous, alas—but do not underestimate its rewards."

"Your prognostications are a trifle vague," I commented. "Is that because my future is more uncertain than most?"

"Yes indeed," he replied, with apparent candor. "And in that you ought to reckon yourself a fortunate man. The more uncertain your future is, the more choice you will have in shaping it, both in writing the script of your own drama and improvising when circumstances warrant it."

I suspected that the reassurance in question was a standard part of his script rather than an improvisation, but I didn't really care. I had gradually moved forward, leaning toward him, and he had not moved back, so that distance between me *volto* and his *bauta* was only a matter of inches. I dropped my soft voice to a whisper, and said: "Tell me about the eyes that the Devil enabled Pietro Beroviero to make in Murano for Bartolomeo Collatino, nine-and-thirty years ago."

I was trying to surprise him. There is always a particular amusement to be derived from startling those who claim to have privileged knowledge of the future. In this instance, I failed. There was not the slightest convulsion in the hand that held mine, and the other had already paused in its exploration of my palm, apparently having exhausted the information contained in its lines.

"Ah," he said, lowering his own voice, "that is a good story. But may I ask who sent you to me to have it told?"

"I don't know the lady's name," I said, "but she gave me a message for you, which will presumably enable you to identify her. She said, if I can remember her exact words: *Tell him that the lady would dearly like possession of the Portals of Paradise to be settled by negotiation, and that he has her guarantee of safe conduct if be cares to come to the Teatro Festim on the Eve of Lent.*"

"Ah," he said again. "And why, may I ask, did she select you to be her messenger?"

"Because she said that you would read in my hand that I am an honest man. She has confidence in your art."

He laughed, briefly. "Does she, indeed? Well, I suppose that I have confidence in *her* art, if not in her word. She has been away from Venice for a long time, and it seems that she has come back in a humor very different from the one in which she went away. Has she asked you to give the same message to any others, by any chance?"

"As a matter of fact, she did," I told him, "but I do not know that I shall see the man in question again before the performance of *Il Re giallo*, to which he has invited me."

This time, I had succeeded in startling him, and the hand that was holding mine twitched convulsively—but without inflicting any damage on me. "Well," he muttered, in Italian, " if it is the man I suspect, I do not think she has much chance of making peace with *him*."

"You know who he is, then?" I queried.

"Don't you?" he countered.

"He said he was the Devil."

Again, Mercutio laughed, in a conspicuously hollow fashion. "That he is, if my suspicions are correct," he said, "and so is she, for sure. You've been keeping dangerous company, my friend—but if I read your hand correctly, you've done so innocently, and you should have nothing to fear. No one means you any harm—including me, if you're anxious about that. Do you know who the person is who claims to have the true eyes?"

"No," I said.

"He must be a clever rogue, to have persuaded her to lend herself to this farce, and to send such messages to me and to the man who's sworn to kill her—but the trickster is playing a dangerous game, probably more dangerous than he realizes, and he'll be lucky to get out of Venice in one piece, whether he collects a reward for his supposed discovery or not. Evidently, he's a man who doesn't believe in the Devil. They call that Enlightenment nowadays, do they not? You can appreciate the irony, I hope, Signor…?"

He left the question mark dangling. It was a relief of sorts finally to meet someone who didn't already know who I was.

"Bowlands," I supplied. "Gabriel Bowlands, of Bristol."

"Good. Thank you, Signor, for bringing me the message. If you happen to see her again, please tell her that I'll take the matter under consideration."

"You haven't answered my question," I pointed out. "I paid Arlecchino his fee, did I not?"

Had he had the power of sight, I might be able to say that he looked up. At any rate, he raised his face so that the single ray of candlelight that escaped the smoked glass caught the polished jet of both glass eyes again. It was as if there were two tiny flames deep within his inner being—not so much in the eyes themselves as the interior of his skull, or the profundity of his soul.

"You want to know the legend from the very source, my lord?" he asked, with a sarcastic edge to his tone.

"I do. I'm a playwright in search of inspiration, as you've already read in my hand," I told him. "I know my Goldoni and my Gozzi, but I'm eager to hear what Venice can offer in the way of drama—or tragedy."

"Tragedy?" he echoed, his voice like velvet. "There is no tragedy in Venice, my lord. There is only comedy. There is Goldoni's comedy, which is all mistakes and misfortunes; there is Gozzi's comedy, which is all fantasy and fabulation; and there is also the Devil's comedy."

I was wary of reading too much into the last remark, but could hardly avoid asking: "And what is the Devil's comedy?"

"All lust," he said, and hesitated for a moment before adding: "and bargains." I could not tell whether he hesitated because he had cast about for an alliterative term and failed to find one, or because did not want to pronounce the word *lies*.

"Does the genre include *Il Re giallo*?" I asked.

"Very probably," he said, with a slight sigh. "We shall both find out, it seems, on the Eve of Lent. You say that you know your Goldoni, Signor Bowlands. Do you know *Il Cavaliere e la Dama*?"

"Yes," I said. "It is a play about cicisbei—martyrs to gallantry, he calls them, and slaves to feminine caprice."

"Well, Signor," he said. "Bartolomeo Collatino was a cicisbeo, and Pietro Beroviero was the father of Bartolomeo's Dama, Caterina di Mastropietro…."

I ought to explain, before going any further, that the follies of courtly and chivalric romance had come a trifle late to the Republic of Venice, long after the death of the last Provençal troubadour, and long after the cities of the Italian mainland had developed their own complex and jealous amorous codes. As recently as a few decades before my Grand Tour, the wives of Venetian patricians were treated in much the same way as those of their great enemies the Turks, locked away in secret apartments—but as the city gradually gave itself over to the year-round riot of festivals, the sternness of solid walls and the guardianship of eunuchs had given way to the delicacy of the carnival mask and the gallantry of cavaliers.

Because the regular society of the Venetian patricians had no place for wives, the wives who began to go abroad made their own society, exclusive of the old routines into which their husbands' conventional way of life had fallen. It swiftly became fashionable for every wife to adopt a *cavalier servente*, or cicisbeo, ostensibly as a helper and protector, and to drag him everywhere—to the theater, to the houses of her friends, even to church. Ostensibly, of course, he waited patiently outside the confessional in the last-named circumstance while the lady made her confession, and did not figure therein at all, but it is probable that he heard those same confessions in his turn, in far more detail and far less censoriously. That, at least, is what the legends that sprang up overnight claimed—although one inevitably sees the hand of poets and dramatists in the forging of those legends, as one does in the making of any modern legendry.

I ought perhaps to add that in reality, many such companions were old and wise rather than young and handsome, and more than a few really were the displaced aristocrats they mostly claimed to be, but that made no difference to the fact that within the space of a century Venice saw the growth of a new legendary and literary tradition in which the stereotyped role of the *cavalier servente* was to serve his idol much as the French Lancelot served the English Queen Guinevere, being more ambitious to play Don Juan than Don Quixote. In that that same *avant garde* folklore, it was not uncommon for the alleged aristocrats playing their new role to turn out to be *bravi* in disguise.

And it was a "modern legend" of that kind that Mercutio the Cheiromancer told me, succinctly and fluently, with the ease of a man well used to spinning stories and constructing narratives.

The blind man with the velvet voice told me that that Caterina di Mastropietro, the Dama of Bartholomeo Collatino—he warned me to beware of words like "mistress", which are so easily mistranslated and misunderstood—was the daughter of Pietro Beroviero, the master glassmaker of Murano, and felt entitled in consequence to consider herself an aristocrat of sorts. The Beroviero family was one of the most powerful in Murano, which had its own Great Council and Golden Book in those days, because the glass-blowers were—and still are—so vital to the wealth of Venice that their microcosm mirrored the greater unity of which it is a part. The Mastropietro family, on the other hand, was one of the most august in the Republic proper, and, from their point of view, at least, the marriage between Leandro di Mastropietro and Caterina Beroviero was seen a matter of reckless condescension at best, and perhaps a matter of entrapment, secured by the lure of uncommon beauty.

Unusually for the time, both Leandro di Mastropietro and Caterina Beroviero were young, and theirs was a love match, not a matter of arrangement between the families, and although the Berovieros were indulgent to Caterina's whim, the Mastropietros were less so of Leandro's, so there was a certain friction, if not an outright animosity, between the two families from the very start.

Leandro was an exceptionally handsome young man, and very vain, as well as politically ambitious. His political ambitions kept him fully occupied in social circles in which women had no role, so Caterina naturally found her own place in the female society of the time, in which a cicisbeo was necessary. Leandro saw no cause to be jealous of his wife's cicisbeo, because he could not imagine that she could ever prefer Bartolomeo to him, Bartolomeo being ten years older than he was and a great deal plainer—but that did not prevent him from slight resentment of the fact that Caterina should feel the need for a cicisbeo at all. According to the blind man, Leandro would rather have lived a hundred years earlier, when a wife could be securely imprisoned from any sight but her husband's.

"What about Collatino's family?" I interjected, at that point. "What was Bartolomeo, apart from being a cicisbeo?" I admit that I was being provocative, for I had already formulated the hypothesis that Mercutio the Blind Cheiromancer might be none other than Bartolomeo Collatino grown old.

"That isn't important," the man with eyes of jet assured me. "Whatever he was before he was a cicisbeo was forgotten, at least by him, as soon as he became one. He played the part to the full, as energetically as any of his peers. As a servant he seemed exceedingly assiduous, as a guide exceedingly reliable, as a listener exceedingly attentive, as a guardian exceedingly dutiful...and as a friend, imperishably loyal. Everyone said that he had no eyes for anyone but his Dama: a comic figure, in a way, who might easily have been a player in a skit by Goldoni, who had forgotten that he was merely acting a part and had continued to improvise…indefinitely, incessantly, and perhaps absurdly."

The cheiromancer's voice had almost faded away, but he collected himself. He told me that whispers had been put about—as seemingly sourceless as such whispers always are—to the effect that Leandro di Mastropiero had been played for a fool twice over, once in marrying beneath him and again in being persuaded to place his wife in the care of a masquerader. That rumor was borne to Leandro's ear by a good friend, Maurizio Scamozzi, who also happened to serve as cicisbeo to Leandro's sister Zulietta, who was married to Andrea Zellini.

By that point in the story I was beginning to find the welter of names of relationships more than a trifle confusing, but the pace of Mercutio's narration had speeded up and as obviously following a well-worn track. I refrained from further interruptions, and simply did my best to commit the names to memory.

Apparently, Zulietta was no friend to Caterina, to whom she always referred as *the bead princess*, because the branch of the Beroviero to which she belonged was the backbone of the bead-makers guild, and her influence, filtered through Maurizio Scamozzi, was a highly significant factor in sowing discord between Leandro and Caterina.

The rumors blackening his wife's name were just as effective in blackening Leandro's mood, and he grew morose—but he was vain enough that the fact that the rumors were circulating troubled him more deeply than the possibility that they might be true. He wanted them stamped out, and he asked his friend to help him put a stop to them. Alas, denial is to rumor what oil is to a conflagration and Leandro became suspicious soon enough that people were laughing behind their hands as they watched him pass by, and was not entirely mistaken. Perhaps unwisely, he swore that he would fight anyone who was heard by a witness to make any slighting remark about his wife or her cavalier. He was forced to take up his sword twice within the week; he wounded both his opponents, and was fortunate not to attract the attention of the Inquisitors.

"Perhaps Leandro became desperate then," the blind man went on, "or perhaps his friend Maurizio, urged on by Zulietta, took it upon himself to save the situation. I do know, though, that a bravo was hired: a reckless young man who called himself Tondino, after the gambling game *tondina*. He *was* a gambler, that Tondino, who delighted in ensnaring his victims in crooked games and wagering for pounds of flesh, all bloodshed included. Even within the guild of *bravi* he was considered something of a dangerous hothead.

Some say that the game of chance that Tondino played with Leandro di Mastropiero one fateful night was a deceit from beginning to end, cooked up in conspiracy between the two of them, while others claim that Leandro was the dupe of his sister, or his friend, or both…but in all probability, only the Devil, Leandro and Tondino know the truth. Perhaps the first plan was to inveigle Bartolomeo into the game, and when that failed, improvisation took over…but however the masquerade was worked, and whoever was pulling the strings, a situation was produced in which Leandro, with his wife and her cicisbeo looking on, was provoked into a bet that was extremely unwise."

"He pledged his eyes?" I asked, racing to get ahead of the plot.

"No," said Mercutio the Cheiromancer. "He was goaded into betting a ring that had been given to him by the father of his bride, and was a significant element of her dowry. It was gold, with a roseate stone shaped like a heart to which no man could put a name, and it was said to be an amulet of considerable power, supposedly gifted to Pietro Beroviero by the Devil because Pietro had once favored the Devil with an act of kindness, and had received it in return."

"But it was really only a trinket?" I prompted.

"Who can tell? At any rate, Leandro's finger had increased in size since the day of his betrothal, and he had already let it slip to his friend Maurizio that the ring was now so tight on his finger that he did not think it could possibly be removed without cutting through the base. Tondino knew that—as did Bartolomeo."

"But how do we progress from there to Bartolomeo's eyes?" I demanded, having lost track of what seemed to me to be the natural trajectory of the plot. "The wager was lost, presumably, and Leandro was asked for the forfeit—and Caterina intervened, I suppose, because the ring meant as much to her as to him even if the finger did not. But…"

"She intervened in the only way she could," the blind man said, his voice a mere whisper. "She asked for time, so that all possible ingenuity might be employed to dislodge the ring that was lost from the finger to which it was clinging so stubbornly. Tondino granted her twenty-four hours. Doctors were summoned, and magicians, and Pietro Beroviero exercised all his diabolical art…but the ring could not be budged.

"So, in the end, Bartolomeo went to meet Tondino, with instructions to buy him off…or to do whatever else might be required to save the situation, including killing him. What happened when they met remained a mystery to everyone but them. Bartolomeo was found two days later, unconscious in a skiff drifting on the Grand Canal. His eyes had been put out. Nothing more was seen or heard of Tondino.

"Leandro di Mastropiero's finger remained intact for a little while, but not for long. His finger was severed one night while he slept too soundly, after being drugged, and rumor put the blame squarely on Tondino, but Tondino could not be found, and nor could the ring—which now appeared, as you suggested earlier, to have been a mere trinket, with no protective power. Whether that was true or not, Leandro certainly did all he could to recover it, putting a price on Tondino's head—but no one ever collected it."

"And in the meantime, Caterina asked her father to make a pair of glass eyes for her wounded cicisbeo?" I suggested, still hastening towards a denouement I thought, once again, that I now could see clearly enough.

"A blind cicisbeo is no cicisbeo at all," the cheiromancer told me. "He must perforce seek other employment—but yes, Bartolomeo seemed to be owed a debt that was greater than any Venetian noblewoman could easily pay. Her father was privy to the darkest secrets of his guild, and also on friendly terms with the Devil. Some say that he complained to the Devil that the amulet that he had given his son-in-law was plainly defective, and that the Devil had cheated him. However the case was put, though, the Devil promised to make amends, and he enabled Pietro to make two pairs of new eyes for Bartolomeo, one of which was supposed to give the wearer to ability not only to see paradise, but somehow, by virtue of that sight, to live a paradisal existence even on earth. That pair became knows as the Portals of Paradise, and was said to confer powers of paradisal vision even on possessors who retained the use of their own eyes as well."

"And what did the other pair do?" I asked.

"Accounts vary, but the most common story is that they gave the wearer, or even a sighted possessor, the power to communicate with angels and command them to carry messages."

"And what happened to the eyes?"

"Again, accounts vary, but what seems to be certain is that Bartolomeo Collatino did acquire a new pair of eyes, without any appreciable delay, and did claim loudly that they not only allowed him the sight of paradise but to live in a paradisal ecstasy. No one, of course, could check his claim, but it was widely believed, and proclaimed as a miracle, whether inspired by God or the Devil. Whatever the truth of the origin of the eyes, and whatever the truth of the claims made by Bartolomeo about their properties, he was far too lavish in his praise of them and the ecstasy in which they permitted him to dwell. He said too much, and was heard, and believed, by the wrong people—the *bravi*, certainly, and the Inquisitors too, in all likelihood. The eyes rapidly obtained the reputation of being far too precious for their humble purpose. Bartolomeo had them for barely a year before they were stolen. It is, alas, all too easy to steal from a man who is blind—even the eyes from his face."

"He had no Arlecchino then, to keep watch for him?" I said, incautiously, carried away at last by the impetus and imagination of the story.

"Why would you mention an Arlecchino?" he retorted, too softly for me to judge whether or not he was speaking ironically. "Are you, perhaps, confusing Bartolomeo Collatino with me, simply because we both lost our eyes? Please don't—I'm not that old, and was never that stupid. I certainly understand how precious a good pair of false eyes might be, but I can assure you that I have never yet had the opportunity to wear the Portals of Paradise."

"I'm sorry," I said. "You seemed so involved with the telling of the story that I assumed that you must have had a part in it."

"My friend," he said, softly, "I know of a dozen blind men who would pay very dearly for those eyes—so dearly that if one of them suspected that you know where they are, he would capable of having you kidnapped and tortured in the hope that they could steal a march on their rivals. I am not the only one among them—far from it—who cannot hope to compete in an auction for such a prize by means of his purse. You are an honest man, as I know by reading your hand, and I believe you when you say that you do not know who has brought the eyes to Venice that are being offered for sale at the Festim on the eve of Lent— or, more likely being used as bait to draw others supposed custodians of one or other of the four eyes out of hiding—but you ought to be careful about giving the message you have given me to others."

"To the man costumed as the Devil, you mean?"

"If I am right in my suspicion regarding his identity, he might be the only interested party who does not want the eyes, and thus the only one who cannot be bought or tricked, but he is perhaps the most dangerous of all, unless his humor has changed drastically since mention was last heard of him in Venice. Doubtless you too have been promised safe conduct by all and sundry, but take it from one who knows: *none of them is to be trusted.*"

Suddenly, the hand on which my own right hand had merely seemed to be resting had closed about the wrist, and was now holding it tightly—not tightly enough to hurt, as yet, but tightly enough to threaten.

"Does that include you?" I ask him, mildly.

Instantly, he let me go. "The others would doubtless tell you so," he said, "but I have read your hand and I have nothing against you. You are safe from me, because you have nothing I want. You are probably safe from them for the same reason—but I repeat my advice: be careful."

My curiosity was far from slaked. "Will you go to the Festim on the Eve of Lent?" I asked.

"Of course."

"If you cannot afford to bid in any auction," I remarked, "why go?"

He made a slight sound that might have been the ghost of long-dead laughter. "Because I need to know who will win that auction, my friend," he said, "if it actually takes place. I need to hear reliable testimony, if there is any, as to whether or not the offered eyes are genuine… and, if they are genuine, whether they are the Portals of Paradise or the other pair."

"If I'm drawing the correct inference from what you say," I said, "the two pairs of eyes that Pietro Beroviero made must somehow have been separated, and have so far resisted attempts to bring them together in order to test their effects. In the meantime, fake eyes have been manufactured, which have been offered more than once to people intensely interested in acquiring the real ones…if there are, in fact, any real ones, given that the whole story might be a diabolical hoax."

"Your logic is impeccable, Signor Bowlands," Mercutio told me, smoothly. "You know as much of the legend now as anyone knows reliably, and can doubtless draw your own corollaries. But you should go now, my friend. Doubtless I have other customers waiting."

I hesitated, but he had already retreated into the shadows, and his attitude made it plain that the interview was over.

VII

THE DEVIL IN BAGDAD

I stepped out of the tent, obedient to the cheriomancer's evident desire, and began to move away, deep in thought, in the direction of the cathedral. I had not taken half a dozen steps, however, before my way was very firmly blocked by Arlecchino.

"Forgive me for interrupting you, my lord," he said, in English, "and believe that I mean you no harm, but would you be so kind as to tell me who sent you with whatever message that you have just delivered to my master?" The politeness of the words was not matched by the tone in which they were spoken, which seemed redolent with vague threat.

"I don't know," I told him. "I didn't see her face."

"Where did you meet her?"

I hesitated for a long time, bur decided in the end that it was a secret I was not obliged to keep, if it was a secret at all.

"Somewhere in Murano," I said. "That's all I know."

I couldn't see his lips behind his *volto*, so I couldn't tell whether or not he smiled, but he was quick enough to step aside, and say: "Thank you, my lord." Apparently, the location, vague as it was, had told him what he wanted to know.

In spite of the ominous quality of his voice, I did not immediately take up his invitation to go on my way. "But the lady only mentioned the auction," I added. "It was the other who told me about the performance of *Il Re giallo*."

A porcelain *volto* gives nothing away. If his expression changed, I had no inkling of it, even in the eyes that I could glimpse through the black mask painted on the porcelain. I saw his body stiffen, though, and the effort that he put into maintaining the even tone of his voice was clearly audible.

"What other was that, if you don't mind my asking, my lord?" he asked.

"He was costumed as the Devil," I said, as casually as I could, "And said that he prefers the name of Lucifer to others. It means, I believe, *bringer of light*."

"Thank you, my lord," he said, automatically. He was as motionless as a statue.

"May I ask you a question in return?" I asked, trying my utmost not merely to match his feigned politeness but to impart an undertone of mystery. He did not reply, but did not move. I felt entitled to construe that as assent. "What interest do you have in this matter, since you do not seem to me simply serving your master?" I asked, blandly.

"Be careful of asking too many questions, my lord," he said. "There are more things than you imagine that it is better not to know?"

"And why is that?" I asked.

He could simply have pointed out that that was one more question, to which the same principle applied, but he didn't bother. "Ask the Devil," he said. "Save for God, he's probably the only one who knows why the world is as it is, and whether the Portals of Paradise are real."

"What about Bartolomeo Collatino?" I objected. "He seems to be the one man who has worn them, and must know whether or not they're real."

"Ask Bartolomeo, then, if you can find him," said Arlecchino. "And then come back and tell me what he says, for I'd dearly like to have a word with him myself."

That seemed to scotch the hypothesis that Mercutio might be Bartholomeo.

"If I see him, I'll certainly advise him of your interest," I said, sarcastically. "Shall I simply say Arlecchino, or would you care to give me another name?"

"Arlecchino, guardian of Mercutio the Chieromancer, will be quite adequate, my friend," he retired, dropping the contrived politeness, and allowing his voice to exhibit naked hostility. But then his attention seemed to be caught by something behind me, and he abandoned his pose, turned round and went back to the door of Mercutio's tent.

I turned round myself to see what had prompted him to move. The Pierrot who had given me the playbill advertising *Il Diavolo in Badgad* was standing a dozen feet away, looking in my direction. He seemed to have run out of playbills, presumably having distributed his entire stock. He raised his left hand briefly and made a surreptitious beckoning gesture. I walked over to him.

"Be careful of that man, Mr. Bowlands," he said. "The guild is not supposed to exist any longer, but its ghost survives, and it's not safe to tangle with them."

"The guild?" I queried.

"The guild of *bravi*," he supplied. He was already turning away, but

I stopped him; he didn't resist the slight pressure of my hand on his arm.

"Why would a *bravo* be standing guard outside a fortune-teller's tent?" I asked.

Pierrot shrugged his shoulders to indicate his ignorance. "There isn't as much call for their…specialist skills now as there once was, and they make their living as they can. But a man may change masks, and remain the same beneath. Be careful, at any rate—and be sure to come along to the play this afternoon, Signor Bowlands. If Mercutio has been telling you his tale, you'll find it doubly interesting."

"You know that tale that Mercutio tells, then?" I asked him.

"Everybody does," he assured me. "I tell it myself."

"And improvise while you do it, as a true adherent of the *Commedia*?"

"Of course. You really will appreciate our play Signor—perhaps as well as a native Venetian, and surely more than all the other Tourists to whom I have been handing these pieces of paper. I look forward to hearing your opinion of it."

"I'll do my best to live up to your hopes," I said. "When your description says, 'in the manner of Carlo Gozzi,' I presume that means that it's a comedy based on folklore?"

Pierrot laughed softly, the broadness of his smile clearly visible in his white-painted face. "Oh yes, Signor" he said. "It's a folktale comedy, all fantasy and fabulation, lust and diabolical bargaining. I dare not say that the performance will be the highlight of your experience of the carnival of Venice, but I promise you that you will not soon forget it."

"You're appearing in it, of course?"

"Yes, Signor," he said.

"But not in that costume, I presume?"

"No, sir; there is no role within it for poor Pierrot—but you will surely recognize me anyway, this time."

I was not particularly concerned, for the moment, about his role in the play. "If you know that Arlecchino is really a bravo, perhaps you also know whether Mercutio is really a cheiromancer?"

"He has the reputation of being a good judge of men, sir," he replied. "He is always here for the Carnival, although he tours with fairs on the mainland for much of the year. He is said to know his art very well, his sense of touch being far more sensitive than most men's eyes, when it is a matter of discerning the possibilities in the mind that guides the hand."

"But he yearns nevertheless to discover the whereabouts of the Portals of Paradise?"

"Certainly, Signor," Pierrot replied, without any hint of surprise at my asking him the question. "There is not a blind man in Venice, and perhaps not the whole of Italy, who does not know a version of that story, and whether they can believe it or not, the mere idea is enough to make them dream. Sighted men, too, frequently yearn to discover the Portals of Paradise. We hope that our play is timely, in that regard, although we have had to disguise it somewhat, for we do not know how many of the characters in Mercutio's story are still alive."

Unlike him, I could not help starting quite sharply with surprise. "Your play features the Portals of Paradise?" I queried.

"Yes, sir—the tale is oft-repeated, especially at Carnival time, but for the reason I just specified, playmakers have hesitated to adapt it for the stage. That is why we have fused it with apparatus borrowed from Antoine Galland and substituted mythical Bagdad for the Venice of forty years ago. Sometimes, as a practitioner like yourself is well aware, a change of scene is necessary, for satirical or diplomatic purposes. As for the Devil…well, you will surely not be surprised to find that he figures prominently in our version of the tale, although some oral versions are careful to dispatch him to the wings."

"Are you, by any chance, playing the part of the Devil?" I asked him.

"Alas, no," he said. "Although in different costume, I shall be playing true to type, as a victim of unrequited love. I'm sure that I would be capable of playing the Devil were I to be given a chance some day, but Signor Landini is stubborn in casting me as Pierrot."

I almost said that I knew the feeling, but I refrained. All things considered, there is no great difference between finding oneself typecast as an angel and finding oneself typecast as a lovesick clown, but I wasn't sure that the actor would recognize the similarity.

I hazarded a conjecture. "That's the role in which I've seen you before, then?" I said. "I've seen you on the Parisian stage, playing Pierrot, or his equivalent."

He smiled, ruefully. "I don't blame you for not remembering me, Signor," he said. "After all, all Pierrots look alike, and it is their fate to be left on the sidelines, always yearning after Columbina, while Arlecchino sweeps her away. If you'll forgive me, though, Signor, I ought to be on my way now. Time's passing, and I shall need to be at the theater long before you."

"One question, before you go," I said. "What do you know about the Teatrao Festim?"

"It's on Guidecca," he said. "A tragic story. It was recently restored and modernized, but its owners were caught up in one of those financial collapses that are becoming distressingly common in these turbulent times. It never opened, and I fear that it never will."

"It appears to be opening very soon, at least for one night. I've been told that it's showing *Il Re giallo* on the Eve of Lent."

Perhaps it was reckless of me to mention that, especially to an actor who seemed to be at the heart of the theatrical rumor mill in Venice, but I figured that if his company was putting on a play about the Portals of Paradise, he might know a great deal more that would help clear up the cloud of mystery by which I was beset. I had grown used to thinking of him as imperturbable, and I was astonished by the violence of his reaction.

"Oh, don't believe it, Signor!" he exclaimed, with palpable anxiety in his voice. "No one performs that play in Venice—and if by chance it's true, for the love of God don't go. That play drives men mad. Believe me, Signor, avoid it like the plague. Place yourself in our hands, Signor Bowlands, and you'll be delighted…but if someone really has hired the Festim to put on that accursed piece, stay away, for the love of God."

He said no more before he hurried away, but I saw his direction of his gaze as he went, directed at Arlecchino the alleged bravo, or perhaps the tent behind him, where Mercutio the Cheiromancer was sitting in eternal shadow.

I had to make haste myself then, having arranged to meet Uncle Jerome for lunch.

"I can't stay very long," I told him, almost as soon as we sat down. "I'm going to a performance that starts at three."

He rolled his eyes. "It seems to me," he said, "that your obsession is on the verge of becoming unhealthy."

"Nonsense," I said, although what I thought was that he might be speaking more truthfully than he knew. "I met an actor from one of the *Commedia* companies I saw in Paris; they're Venetian in origin and have come home for the Carnival. They're putting on a new comedy." I showed him the playbill that Pierrot had given me.

"*Il Diavolo in Bagdad?*" he queried. "What would the Devil be doing in Bagdad. Do the Mohammedans believe in the Devil?"

"They have their own adversary, called Iblis," I told him. "He's still the Devil, though, albeit in a different costume. Anyway, it's a comedy, and I'm told that the Badgad featured therein is simply Venice, disguised for satirical purposes."

"There are other things in life apart from plays," he told me, for what must have been the thousandth time.

"No, there aren't," I retorted, for at least the five hundredth. "There are plays that are confined by the stage, watched at a safe distance from an armchair or a box, and there are plays performed everywhere else, in which one sometimes finds a role to play, but there isn't anything in life that isn't drama, comedy and tragedy, partly scripted and partly improvised."

"So we're not going to complete our tour today?"

"No. Tomorrow, for sure."

He didn't seem excessively disappointed. "And then we make a plan for the big day?" he said.

"Most of it."

"Because you're going to the theater in the evening>"

"Exactly."

"Well," said Uncle Jerome, "I owe your father a letter anyway, so I'll write one this afternoon—although God only knows when it will reach England. I'll try to be diplomatic in reporting the progress of your education, for my sake as well as yours. I'm sure he'd like me to keep you on a much tighter rein. As for your grandfather..."

"He'd be proud of me," I said, blithely. "After the play on Tuesday, I'll be going to an auction that will add a whole new dimension to the notion of Merchant Adventuring."

"Good," said Uncle Jerome. "Venice was the homeland of Merchant Adventurers for hundreds of years before Bristol became a center of American trade. I'll be sure to tell your father that you're taking an interest in that aspect of the city's life, in spite of its state of advanced decay. Are you thinking of bidding on something—a painting, maybe?"

"No," I reassured him. "I know full well that we're not the kind of Tourists who send back crate after crate of crudely faked Canalettos or knick-knacks for a Cabinet of Curiosities. I'm just going to watch. It should be interesting."

Doubtless I would have told him more if he'd been genuinely interested, but he wasn't. I suspected that he had plans of his own, which had been accelerated by the news at I would be busy in the afternoon as well as the evening.

The theater for which I was headed was in Cannaregio, near the Ponte dell Guglie, the so-called Bridge of Spires, I found it easily enough., and obtained a box without any difficulty, even though it was only a matter of minutes before the curtain was due to go up. The audience seemed conspicuously sparse, the theater being only half full, but the boxes had fewer vacancies than the armchairs down below, undoubtedly being populated almost entirely by Tourists.

I scanned the array of masks reflexively, not expecting to obtain any significant information from the bland collection of porcelain and the ornate facades of fabric, but my eye was caught by one particular couple diagonally across the hall from my position. I could not have recognized Adelaide Harrington, shielded as she was by a *volta*, but her companion was wearing an obsolete *moretta* with wide eyeholes, and I could see just enough of her face to be certain that it belonged to the she-bear, the maiden aunt.

I had no sooner recognized her than she began staring at me, and I realized that my blond hair and characteristic clothing had given me away in spite of my own *volto*. She knew that it was me, and might well have heard that Uncle Jerome had been asking around about her presence in Venice, for her attitude was clearly hostile, and she made no attempt to draw Adelaide's attention to my presence. I inclined my head politely, and then turned away to watch the stage, where the performance was beginning.

Doubtless, if my Italian had been better, I would have understood far more of the dialogue, but colloquial speech is inevitably difficult to follow, and witty wordplay even more so. The scattered audience down below was laughing from the start, but it was noticeable that the people in the boxes, almost without exception, were bewildered. Sometimes they joined in with the laughter, but somewhat half-heartedly.

The plot of the play seemed to have borrowed some of its initial elements from the play by Goldoni that Mercutio the Cheiromancer had mentioned to me, *Il Cavaliere e la Dama*, in that it contained a Dama of sorts—albeit a peri rather than a Venetian noblewoman—and a cicisbeo of sorts in her guardian ogre, but they were not the leading characters. The peri's husband was a human prince, who was delighted to have a peri for his bride, but he too seemed to be playing second fiddle to the central character in the story, that being his envious half-sister, who was—presumably in consequence of a maternal indiscretion—half-Moorish. I gathered that the reason why that bastard offspring was resident in the prince's palace had something to do with a bargain made with the Devil, but its exact terms remained mysterious, at least to me. I was left in no doubt, though, that the dark witch was exceedingly jealous of the peri, and loud in her proclamations that her brother had been bewitched by means of a magic ring that he now wore on his finger.

Unsurprisingly, given the story that Mercutio had told me, I immediately linked the prince with Leandro di Mastropietro, the peri with Caterina, the ogre with Bartolomeo Collatino and the dark witch with Zulietta. Unlike the Zulietta in Mercuitio's story, however, the Moorish witch had neither a husband nor a servant of her own, although she did seem to have a very amicable relationship with the Devil—an actor in a costume eerily similar that of the Devil I had met—with whom she consorted in order to work spells.

As soon as the actor playing the Devil made his first entrance I began watching him intently, with the aid of my lorgnette, trying to work out whether he might be the man I had stumbled over in the back-street in Santa Croce. I did not think he was, but I could not eliminate the possibility entirely from consideration. He was certainly a enthusiastic actor though, and took full advantage of the scope his part gave him for extravagant gestures and declamation.

Although the Mooress had no husband or cicisbeo, she was passionately desired by two typical comic villains, who must have met her long before the play began, under circumstances that were unclear to me, one of whom was identifiable, now that I had seen him at closer quarters and had been forewarned, as the Pierrot to whom I spoken before, He was not easily recognizable, because his character was masked, but I knew that it was him.

The comic villains also seemed to be more important to the plot of the play than the prince or the ogre. The ex-Pierrot was a pirate, the other a brigand, and before the introductory act was done they had conducted an absurd competition in which they tried to out-do one another in complimenting the virtues of the absent witch. It degenerated into a knockabout brawl, but ended with them swearing an alliance, declaring that they would co-operate in every way to make the Mooress captive and then play a game of chance to determine which one would have her, with the loser forfeiting his eyes. By that time, I had changed my mind about the ogre being Bartolomeo Collatino and decided that he must be either the pirate or the brigand—probably the former—while the other was standing in for the *bravo* Tondino.

The bargain struck over the gamble that would cost one of the two lovestruck villains his eyes seemed to me to be the most obvious joke in the opening act, but it was met with a profound silence from the crowd on the floor as well as in the boxes. Perhaps the Venetians in the audience thought the issue a little too sensitive, even after forty years, for such irreverent comedy.

I didn't bother to leave the box during the entr'acte, but a couple of minutes into the interval there was a knock on the door and the manager of the troupe. Signor Landini, came in to shake my hand and tell me how glad he was that Pierrot had managed to cross my path. He asked me how I liked the play, and I was able to reply, with complete honesty, that I found it exceedingly interesting, and very useful to my research.

He seemed suitably delighted, and took the trouble to mention that the Mademoiselles Harrington were also in the audience, Pierrot having found them too in the crowd on the Piazza. Plainly, Adelaide's beauty had made an impression in Paris too—either that or the maiden aunt had attracted attention with a complaint of some sort.

The second act began quite promisingly, from my own viewpoint, given that I was still searching avidly for parallels with the story I had heard from the cheiromancer. The villainess was spreading slanders against the peri, which seemed to cause the ogre a great deal of pain. It was difficult for me, however, to feel much sympathy for the ogre, whose appearance was bestial and coarsely hairy. The player representing him wore a mask like a gorilla, save only for the horn projecting from its forehead. There did not seem to be any implication that the ogre was anything more than a faithful servant set to guard the peri by her mother, who was a queen among her own folk.

The plot careered along at a hectic pace, as it had to do if it were to finish within the indicated time-span, and I'm not at all sure that I kept up with its finer intricacies. In its broad outline, however, when the pirate and the brigand contrived to carry off the villainess she immediately volunteered to fall in with their scheme if they would agree to steal the ring from the prince's finger. She let them into the palace in order to do it, but when they fell upon the prince they could not prize the ring from his finger, and his cries for help brought the ogre rushing to save him. There ensued another comic battle, involving several men-at-arms as well as the four main protagonists. At the end of it, the ogre lay dead—a fact announced very loudly for the benefit of anyone in the crowd who had not seen him fall or taken the correct inference—and the prince's ring-finger had been severed from his hand, ring and all.

The climax of the play was the settlement of affairs between the pirate, the brigand and the villainess. The Mooress took possession of the ring and established the rules for the game of chance that would determine which of her two suitors would marry her, and which would lose his eyes. At this point, however, the peri queen put in an appearance, exacting a magical vengeance for her ogre by taking back the ring and striking both men blind. As soon as she had made her exit, though, the defiant Mooress called upon the Devil to avenge the insult, and swore that she would still wed the better of the two blind men, if the Devil would provide new eyes for both of them better than the ones they had had before.

Again the Devil came on stage, wearing a costume identical to the one I had seen the previous evening, but in far better repair. He told the witch, seemingly without much enthusiasm, that he would do as she asked, by manufacturing two pairs of seemingly-identical glass eyes, one of which—the one to be given to the loser of the wager, not the winner—would enable the wearer to see and dwell in paradise, while the other would enable an enhanced natural sight with the added advantage of making djinn visible. He warned her, however, to be very careful of his gift, else disaster would ensue.

When the Devil had gone, the blind pirate and the blind bandit played their game of chance, which the pirate won, but in the confusion, the two pairs of glass eyes were mixed up, so that each of the villains received one each, and neither could see anything at all. Each of them accused the other of cheating, and they began fighting again, attempting to pluck out one another's eyes in the attempt to reconstitute a pair. In the meantime, the prince whose finger had been excised came on stage again, accompanied by his peri wife, in pursuit of the Mooress, who was forced to appeal to the Devil to carry her away.

By the time the Devil arrived, however, the pirate and the bandit had each succeeded in plucking out one of his rival's eyes, but neither had been able to hang on to his prize, and both had dropped the eyes they had removed. Both fled when the Devil arrived, and so did the prince, but the prince picked up one of the discarded eyes as he went, while the Mooress picked up the other, with the result that the four were separated and scattered. That seemed to annoy the Devil greatly, and the peri too, who confronted the Devil and charged him with having broken the bargain made before the action of the play began. As a result, the Devil told the Mooress that he would never answer her summons again until she had recovered all four eyes and returned them to him, in order that he could placate the peri and her mother.

At that point—very abruptly and unsatisfactorily, by my esthetic standards—the play ended. The conclusion was, however, greeted with as much applause from the auditorium as the relatively sparse crowd could provide, and the Tourists in the boxes joined in politely, as I did myself. Not unnaturally, my first instinct was to blame my poor Italian for the aspects of the plot of which I could make no sense, but I thought that I ought at least to consult the manager of the troupe or the Pierrot who had handed me the playbill, and seek some clarification.

With that aim in mind I went down to the foyer, and waited there, hoping that I might meet one of them—a hope that was almost immediately answered, as the actor wearing the costume of the pirate, but without the mask, came out into the foyer, evidently looking for me. As soon, as he caught sight of me he came directly toward me and said:

"My dear Signor Bowlands, I hope that you were not disappointed. That was our first performance, as you know, and our improvisations were groping for effect—not entirely successfully, I fear. Given that you seem to be familiar with the legend of the Portals of Paradise, however, I hope that you found the plot easy enough to follow."

"It's a very daring play," I told him, judiciously, "in terms of its pace and complexity, and I admired that greatly. My Italian is, I fear, not as good as my French, and some of the dialogue seemed to require a mastery of Venetian dialect that I do not have, but..."

I never got to add the subsidiary clause, because we were suddenly interrupted by a hurricane in a *moretta* that was anything but *muta*, in spite of the difficulty of speaking—or, rather, fulminating—through the mask.

"Mr. Bowlands!" it raged, "I find it absolutely intolerable that you have followed us here, and are obviously waiting in the foyer to see us leave. I have made it clear to your uncle that I do not want to introduce you to my daughter, and I find your persistence in the face of that rejection annoying in the extreme!"

Behind the maiden aunt I could see a young woman in a *volta* who was making urgent apologetic hand-signals to me. I could no more see her face than she could see mine, but I did not have to see her blush to understand her embarrassment.

I opened my mouth to reply, trying to muster sufficient composure to formulate an explanation, but the task was taken out of my hands, as the actor in the pirate costume stepped in between the termagant and me, and bowed deeply.

"My dear Mademoiselle Harrington," he said, "Eduardo Lucca, at your service. I fear there has been a misunderstanding, which is entirely my fault. I was distributing playbills in the Piazza San Marco this morning, costumed as Pierrot. I recognized you and your niece, having seen you both in the theater in Paris where our company was performing Goldoni, and handed one to your niece. I recognized Mr. Bowlands too, and urged him to come to see the play, because I was enthusiastic to hear the opinion of a man so familiar with the contemporary French stage. He did not follow you here, and the simultaneous presence here of the two young people is purely coincidental."

That stopped the she-bear in her tracks, as she suddenly realized, belatedly, that she had just made a complete fool of herself by virtue of a reckless assumption. She froze, uncertain of what she ought to do or say—and Adelaide took advantage of the unexpected opportunity to step forward.

Addressing the actor, she said: "Thank you, Signor Lucca, for explaining the situation. We're very sorry to have interrupted you unnecessarily." Then, without a glance at her aunt, she turned to me and extended a gloved hand. "I apologize to you too, Mr. Bowlands, and I hope you can forgive us, not merely for the unintended insult but for the belatedness of this introduction. I'm Adelaide Harrington."

Dazedly, I took her hand, raised it to my mouth, inclined my head and brushed the glove with my lips. "I'm delighted to meet you, Miss Harrington," I said. "It appears that we share a liking for the theater."

I could only imagine the elder Miss Harrington's face turning purple, but it was an amusing image. Carlo Gozzi would probably have been proud of the effect had he been able to educate his actors to produce it.

I had to augment the image further, however, when Adelaide replied: "We certainly do, Signor Bowlands, and I shall ask my aunt to invite you and Signor Bowlands senior to tea at our hotel tomorrow, in order that we might discuss it."

And with that, she drew her aunt away. I heard muttering from behind the *moretta* as they went, in which I thought I detected the phrases "moral decay" and "shameless impertinence" and definitely heard the judgment that the elder Miss Harrington "did not know what the world was coming to."

"Well, Signor," said Eduardo Lucca, when they were finally out of earshot, "that seemed to work out quite well, in the end. It is not often that misunderstandings create such opportunities."

"Indeed not," I said, still flabbergasted by which had just happened.

"But that is the essence of comedy, is it not?" the actor added. "The unexpected or the absurd that, once it becomes manifest, suddenly seems to have been inevitable all along."

"It was certainly unexpected," I agreed, without commenting on the alleged inevitability.

"You were, I believe," the actor went on, seamlessly, "about to express some reservation about the play."

"Oh no," I hastened to say, "merely an apology for my own inability to follow it as competently as I would have liked. I was taken by surprise by the fact that the relationships between the leading characters differed quite sharply from the version of the local legend that was reported to me, in which Zulietta—the apparent equivalent of your Mooress—only played a peripheral role."

"Ah!" said Lucca. "That is because the forgers of the local legend never knew the whole story of the conspiracies revolving around the Devil's ring. Even rumor, for once, was found wanting."

"But you do know it?" I queried.

"It would be ambitious to claim that I know the whole story," Lucca admitted, "and there is always room for innovation and improvisation when one adapts familiar stories, but yes, I do believe that I know more than most."

"From what source?"

"The Devil."

"The Devil?"

"The actor who plays the Devil in the comedy, that is—and one of the principal authors of the script."

"The other being you?"

Eduardo Lucca bowed. "I have that honor," he confirmed.

My immediate impulse was to ask him whether he would introduce me to his co-author, in order that I could at least compare his voice with that of the individual I had tripped over in the back street, but I knew that it wouldn't make the question of their possible identity any easier to solve. In any case, my time was limited, as I had further plans for the evening, and I only had a few minutes to spare for the present conversation.

The news that my interlocutor was the co-author of the play also made me doubly anxious about venturing any further comment that might be construed as a criticism, but after a moment's hesitation, as he was evidently avid to hear further comment, I thought I might risk one more observation. "The ending seems a trifle inconclusive," I said, trying to make it sound like an expression of curiosity rather than a complaint.

"As is true to the original legend," the actor was quick to say. "That is how the story goes. One way or another, the eyes were separated and scattered. Zulietta never managed to reassemble them, although she certainly tried hard, and was never exactly sure who possessed them. Bartolomeo and Tondino each had one to begin with, but rumor contends that neither had it in his possession when Andrea Zellini caught up with them. Apparently, the *bravi*, led by Maurizio Scamozzi, got to them ahead of him, but if so, Scamozzi certainly did not return the eyes to Zulietta. The one that Leandro had is said to have been reclaimed by the Berovieros at some stage, but he never recovered his ring. What happened to the ring and the eye Leandro had, no one seems to know. Since then, if anyone has ever managed to obtain two of Pietro's eyes at the same time, they do not seem to have constituted a pair. Given that, it was not possible for our play to present a more definite conclusion; any such denouement would seem to the Venetian section of the audience to be blatantly false."

"I see," I said. "It's strange—forty-eight hours ago I had never heard of this particular Venetian legend, but since arriving here, I have heard of little else."

"Legends take time to spread," the actor told me. "This one was only formulated thirty-and-some years ago—time enough to become familiar in Venice, and perhaps a part of the northern mainland, but the people of Florence or Rome would probably dismiss it as trivia of no interest, whereas Venetians regard it as their own, almost as a matter of personal interest. Future literary versions will doubtless struggle in a similar fashion with the seeming inconclusivity of the denouement."

"Unless, of course," I mused, "a conclusion could yet be contrived."

"Too late, I fear," said the actor. "Most of the characters in the actual drama must be dead by now, and any secrets they were carrying regarding what really happened probably died with them. In any case, there is an esthetics of uncertainty as well as one of neatness, is there not. Signor Bowlands? While the Portals of Paradise are still thought to exist, separated and incapable of function, they still function as a lure, a tempting notion. They have been offered for sale several times in the last thirty-nine years, so it's said, one or two at a time, but the purchasers have always been disappointed...thus extending the legend."

"As they doubtless will be again," I said, looking him in his unmasked eyes to judge his reaction. "At the Teatro Festim, apparently."

He shook his head vigorously. "No, no," he said. "When you asked me about the Festim, I asked around the company. There have been whispers it seems. *Il Re giallo* as a prelude to reunion of all four of Pietro's eyes, if their various possessors can only be tempted to attend! That, my friend, is more than a footnote to the legend. It cannot be true, but if it is, you must not go, Signor. No matter how curious you are, believe me, that is one play you must never try to see."

I wondered what he might say if I told him that I had received an invitation to the performance, and a guarantee of my safety, from an individual representing himself as the Devil, but I did not attempt the experiment, lest he think that I had already been driven mad by the mere mention of the King in Yellow. I was becoming increasingly conscious of the need to hurry away, but there were still a host of questions that I wanted to ask.

Instead of making my apologies and taking my leave, therefore, I said: "There are whispers, you say? The rumor is spreading, then?"

"This is Venice, my friend, and the Carnival. There are always whispers of the supernatural in the air, and talk of the Devil...sufficient, perhaps, to keep sensible people well away from the Festim until Lent begins…but to attract madmen."

By "madmen," I assumed that he meant those mad enough to believe that they possessed one of Pietro's eyes, as well as those avid to acquire them.

"In Paris," I said, "the mere whisper of a performance of *Le Roi en jaune* would guarantee that there would be a full house, and not of lunatics."

"No, Signor," said the actor, "it would merely draw a few dozen pretended *philosophes* eager to put their spiritual armor to the test. Theater folk are very superstitious, and even in Paris, the legend of *Le Roi en jaune* is taken more seriously than you might imagine. Here, as I warned you earlier, there is also the guild to fear, and their vendettas. Believe me, Signor, you must not yield to the temptation of whatever you have heard."

"I can't quite see how the guild of *bravi* are involved in the legend of the Portals of Paradise," I admitted, "and why they would still be interested, if they really do still exist."

"Tondino and Maurizio Scamozzi were both important guildsmen, close friends or perhaps secret rivals, in spite of the difference in their ages. They both disappeared. One way or another, that interested the guild thirty-nine years ago, and it still interests them today. If the Portals of Paradise really have returned to Venice, after all these years, the *bravi* will want to know who has them, and where they have been since Bartolomeo Collatino's were put out."

"But they're not interested in the supposed magical properties of the eyes?"

"As to that, I wouldn't know—but I do know that the mystery of what happened to Tondino and Scamozzi still irks them."

"As a proud *philosophe*," I commented, "I suppose I ought not to be intrigued myself by the idea of the Portals of Paradise—but I can understand why Mercutio the Cheiromancer might be prepared to hope, if not to believe."

"Was it Mercutio who told you about the Teatro Festim?"

"No. He only told me the story of Bartolomeo Collatino."

"He's done as much as anyone to keep the legend alive. He's obsessed with the story—for understandable reasons, as you say. If you are right about the performance at the Festim—and I pray that it is merely an empty rumor—Mercutio will go, but whether Arlecchino in is hireling or his keeper, his blindness might not protect him from a thrust of a stiletto, any more than it can shield him from the madness of *Il Re giallo*."

"When he began to tell me the story, I thought he might actually be Bartolomeo Collatino."

"No, Signor, he's not old enough—Bartolomeo would be over eighty if he were still alive. Given the condition of his eyes, though, it's an understandable error."

"You seem to have eliminated the character from your version, or at least divided him in two, as the ogre and the pirate."

"Two characters were more convenient than one, in terms of our narrative."

"And his version gave a greater priority to Pietro Beroviero's alchemical art than the Devil."

"Really? We never considered that possibility. For us, the Devil is the key to everything—but we're working in the Gozzi manner, after all. Mercutio is probably a Goldoni man through and through. That's not surprising in a hand-reader, even one who would dearly like to believe in the Portals of Paradise."

"Perhaps not," I agreed. "I fear that I really must go now; I no longer even have time for a rapid meal before the next performance begins."

"Oh? Which performance?"

"Goldoni, I fear—*Il Servitore di due padrone*."

"Ah—an old favorite, and a masterpiece. A much more prestigious company than ours. You'll appreciate it enormously. I hope you won't forget us entirely, though."

"Certainly not," I said. "You've done me an enormous favor, in enabling my introduction to Miss Harrington. I'll be eternally grateful."

"It seems to me that she enabled it herself," he observed, "but if I've helped, I'm glad." Eduardo Lucca extended his hand for me to shake, and I clasped it briefly as I beat an overdue retreat.

Inevitably, as soon as I had left the theater I began to thinking of other questions that I might have asked him, about the legend of the Portals of Paradise, but I forgave myself rapidly enough. I had, after all, increased what I already knew by a factor of three or four, even if much of the increase was a tangle of rival fictions, with no kernel of truth clearly in sight, and none likely to come into sight until the various actors took off their masks—if they ever did, and if there was anything behind their masks but further masks.

VIII

A LICENSE TO DEAL WITH THE IMPOSSIBLE

When I got back to the hotel after the performance of *Il Servitore di due padrone*, I half-expected to find that Uncle Jerome was out in pursuit of his own pleasures, or suffering from a surfeit of wine, but in fact, he was present, sober and in a state of strangely gleeful excitement.

"Guess what I've received while you were out!" he challenged me, exultantly.

"An invitation to tea with the Harringtons," I answered, calmly.

"Oh," he said, suddenly deflated. "You know."

"Yes," I said. "Adelaide Harrington introduced herself to me this afternoon, taking advantage of a blunder on her aunt's part that briefly gave her the upper hand in their contest of wills. The she-bear doubtless considered it unacceptably forward of her, but I suspect that Adelaide has been Touring long enough to become heartily sick of the old woman, and has been getting ready to throw propriety overboard for a month. You might have to entertain the old dragon, I fear, or at least keep her cornered, while Adelaide and I exchange views on the theater. It's bound to be a chore, but I'll be eternally grateful."

"You're welcome," said Uncle Jerome. "Just don't let this opportunity fizzle out like the last one."

"The last one wasn't an opportunity," I told him. "And in any case, I suspect that I might run into the dark lady again."

"At the mysterious auction you mentioned?"

"Indeed."

"She'll be there?"

"I suspect so."

"Oh—well, in that case, you ought to know that she's not who we originally thought."

"Not the widow Senedes, you mean?"

"Correct. Apparently, the widow Senedes is no longer in Venice. She's returned to Florence."

"Who's living in her apartment, then?" I asked, unable for the moment to see where this unexpected extra piece might fit into the bewildering puzzle but also unable to see that it mattered greatly, as I had already rejected the hypothesis that the dark lady might be the widow in question.

"Only a skeleton domestic staff."

"You mean that the lady in the moretta was her chambermaid?"

"Not even that. According to the hotel staff, there are no female residents there at all. According to them, in fact, the lady on the balcony was a ghost."

"A ghost?" I echoed, altering my estimation of the possible significance of the new item of information.

"Yes. She's been seen before, apparently, always during Carnival."

"Whose ghost?"

"Nobody knows."

Skepticism, momentarily stirred, reasserted its empire. "A ghost who writes letters?" I asked, sarcastically. "A ghost who arranges assignations? She seemed solid enough while I was with her. We both drank wine. I didn't actually touch her, but she certainly seemed substantial to me."

"I'm only telling you what the hotel staff told me. I don't believe in ghosts any more than you do. Whoever was playing the part, though, it wasn't the widow Senedese or her maid."

I nodded. "Playing the part," I echoed, pensively. "That's what she was doing. Just like the Devil…and Pierrot too. They're all playing parts. The question is, why? What's the plot? What denouement can there be…if any is possible at all?"

"No," said Uncle Jerome, "the question is: what the hell are you blithering about?"

It was late, but the possibility of simply going to bed and sleeping seemed remote. I had far too much to think about. My instinct still told me to keep the matter to myself, but there seemed to be no rational reason for doing so, and as my supposed mentor, Uncle Jerome probably deserved an explanation. At the very least, if I delayed giving him one for much longer, he would be seriously annoyed when I finally did.

"I seem to have been drawn into a sequel to a local legend," I told him. "I have no idea why, or what's expected of me, but various parties seem to want me to be a part of it."

"Do I need to repeat the question?" Uncle Jerome asked.

"No," I said. "I'll bring you up to date."

So I sat him down, and told him, succinctly, about my seemingly-accidental encounter with the individual costumed as the Devil, my meeting in Murano with the balcony "ghost," my consultation with

Mercutio the Cheiromancer, my conversation with Eduardo Lucca, and the bizarre tale of the artificial eyes known as the Portals of Paradise and their alleged counterparts.

"Damn!" he said, when I'd finished. "I've heard some peculiar things in my time, but that beats them all by a country mile."

"I should think so," I agreed. "Sleep on it, and let me know if you've got any ideas in the morning."

As I'd anticipated, it was difficult to get to sleep, and although telling the story to Uncle Jerome had given me a sense of relief, and an impression of sharing the burden of puzzlement, it didn't let me off my own hook. It would, I suppose, be convenient if we really could delegate our confusion when it reached the point of overload, but inviting Uncle Jerome to think about it didn't liberate me from the necessity of thinking about it myself, any more than Carlo Goldoni had been able to provide sufficient distraction to deflect my attention earlier in the evening. The play was a masterpiece, the company first rate, but my heart simply hadn't been in it. When I took the enigma to bed, I was even beginning to wonder whether tea with Adelaide Harrington would be adequate to provide me with an alternative preoccupation, and also to worry about the possibility that she would perceive my distraction and misinterpret it.

Where Goldoni had failed in the evening, the remainder of Uncle Jerome's guided tour had no chance at all on the Monday morning. We completed it, for form's sake, but we were both just going through the motions, and I no longer felt the slightest entitlement to criticize the city and the Carnival for doing the same. We didn't even bother to begin discussing plans for more detailed consultation of the city's monuments and galleries.

Uncle Jerome did, however, want to make at least one plan when we stopped to eat a leisurely midday meal.

"You're not going to this supposedly maddening play on your own," he told me, firmly. "If I'm not with you, you don't budge from the hotel room—is that clear?"

"The Devil told me to come alone," I objected, mildly.

"Damn the Devil. If there's going to be trouble at this auction of glass eyes, I want to be there to get you out of it."

I remembered, then, the most important reason why I had refrained for so long from telling Uncle Jerome what was going on, but it was far too late to repent of the previous night's decision and seal my mouth retrospectively.

"I'm supposed to be in a box," I said, with a sigh. "Hopefully, there'll be room to squeeze in an extra chair, and I expect the doorman will let us both in on my pass."

"Good—that's settled. Now, explain to me exactly how this play is supposed to drive men mad?"

"It's just a theatrical legend," I said. "The play doesn't actually exist, except in the sense that, ever since the legend began, there's been a strong temptation to invent it. Whatever is put on tomorrow will be one more attempt to fill the gap. The only way it will drive anyone mad is by trying their patience to breaking point by making them wait for the auction—if there is an auction. If I'm reading the situation correctly, the organizers wanted to keep the crowd small and select, serious bidders only, and they wanted especially to keep out potential trouble-makers, who couldn't bid but might want to acquire the goods by violent means. If that possibility has evaporated, allowing the guild of *bravi* to become seriously involved, the sellers might decide that a new strategy is in order."

"Unless, of course," Uncle Jerome pointed out, "that is their strategy: to build up expectation, stir up a fight…and then auction the goods secretly at a later date, having generated a situation where a buyer might not be able to inspect the fakes too closely beforehand."

"Perhaps," I agreed.

"But you don't think so?"

"No. Some of what's happened, at least, has been pure coincidence rather than contrivance. I can't believe that it was supposed to get this messy. There are several conflicting agendas at work here, and at least some of the contending parties are taking the matter very seriously. Obviously, I don't say that the Portals of Paradise really can enable their possessor to dwell in paradise, but some of the people who are after them surely believe that they can, and are willing to make strenuous efforts to acquire them."

He shrugged his shoulders. "If you say so," he conceded. "Why is this imaginary play called *The King in Yellow?*"

"According to the legend, the climatic scene of the play is set at a masked ball, and the title is generally thought to refer to one of the costumes—except that it isn't a person in costume, but a horrible and destructive supernatural entity of some kind, probably the Devil, or one of the Devil's minions. It's the sight of that entity that is supposed to drive people mad."

"And what's the mythical play's connection with the magic eyes?"

"There's no connection between the two legends, so far as I know… but there is a certain logic to the decision to auction the Portals of Paradise in the context of a play featuring an image supposed to drive spectators mad."

That logic wasn't immediately obvious to Uncle Jerome, but he hadn't had as long to think about it as I had. "What do you mean?" he asked.

"If one assumes that people able to believe in the Portals of Paradise are also able to believe in the baneful power of *The King in Yellow*, that context might deter sighted people from attending, but not the blind, who would have nothing to fear from the demon, while being the ones who stand to gain most from possession of the glass eyes."

Uncle Jerome shook his head. "It's ludicrous," he said.

I couldn't disagree. The whole affair was ludicrous: a comedy in the manner of Gozzi, not Goldoni.

"Given the Decadent age we live in," Uncle Jerome added, "putting on a supposed performance of this legendary play is more likely to attract spectators than deter them, some as an irresistible challenge to their skepticism and their sanity, others as an appeal to their perversity."

"It might, as you say, attract hard-headed and jaded Tourists and *philosophes*—people who not only can't believe that a pair of glass eyes might open a path to paradisal existence, but who can't even believe any longer in any kind of paradisal existence. As for native Venetians, though, I'm not so sure. Eduardo Lucca's company is willing to put on a comedy based on the legend of the glass eyes, albeit safely transplanted into a context borrowed from the Arabian Nights, but whether any of them would risk appearing in, or even attending, a performance of *Il Re giallo* is a different matter."

"That's something else I don't understand," my uncle objected. "Why did the Devil or the alchemist make two sets of eyes, if there was only one blind man in need of them?"

"I don't know," I said. "The writers of *Il Diavolo in Bagdad* seem to have decided that there were two blind men, and Mercutio's version leaves room for that possibility. On the other hand, the second pair of eyes might have been introduced into the legend as it was initially formulated as a secondary elaboration, added in order to provide an explanation of sorts of why it had been so difficult to locate the Portals of Paradise in the past, and why the artifacts offered for sale in the past have proved disappointing. The other pair don't seem to be coveted as intensely as the Portals of Paradise, so they're probably irrelevant to whatever might happen on Tuesday. The embellishment of that idea in *Il Diavalo in Bagdad* is probably of no significance, unless…" I stopped because the "unless" had slipped out, in response to something that had only just occurred to me, and which, as soon as I began to think about it, seemed to require more careful consideration.

Uncle Jerome, however, wasn't known for his patience. "Unless what?" he demanded.

"Unless the actor wearing the Devil costume in *Il Diavolo in Bagdad* really was the same person that I tripped over in that side-street near San Giacomo dell'Orio," I said, hedging rather than answering the question.

"But said just now that you thought he wasn't. On the other hand, the man you tripped over knew about the performance at the theater on Giudecca, so he'd obviously heard the same whispers your Pierrot mentioned to you."

"Except," I said, "that the Devil seemed to think that he was doing me a big favor by telling me about the performance, whereas Pierrot's only impulse was to urge me not to go."

While speaking, I rummaged in my pocket and brought out the sheet from my notebook on which the Devil had scribbled the address of the Teatro Festim and the mysterious line of unfamiliar characters that was supposed to get me in. I showed them to Uncle Jerome. "Do you have any idea what language that might be?" I asked him.

"None at all," he said. "It looks a little like Greek, but it's not."

"No," I agreed, "It's not." I was careful then not to leave the opening of a further sentence dangling, because the idea that I was trying to follow through in my mind was too ludicrous for words, and it certainly wasn't anything that I could explain to my uncle.

"It seems to me," he said, "that the mystery woman from the balcony must have been in collusion with the fellow costumed as the Devil. In fact, they might both be actors from the same troupe as this Lucca fellow, and the whole thing might be an elaborate joke they've cooked up—God alone knows why."

"That might be the explanation that makes most appeal to common sense," I agreed, "although it's hard to believe that they'd go to so much trouble, unless you're paying them, having come up with some crazy plan to cure me of my fascination with the theater..."

"I wouldn't be so stupid," Uncle Jerome assured me—and I believed him.

"...But I can't believe it," I continued. "I think the mystery woman was genuinely astonished when I mentioned the Teatro Festim to her, and genuinely confused. If my encounter with the Devil wasn't a coincidence, as it surely wasn't, then someone is playing games with her as well as me. Mercutio, I think, is serious, at least in his obsession, and he can't be the only one. There are people who really do believe in the Portals of Paradise and want to acquire them fervently—which means that whoever is trying to sell them needs to be very careful. I thought at first that the woman on the balcony might be a seller, who wanted me to get the message to Mercutio in order the bring a potential buyer to the auction, but that doesn't make sense."

"Doesn't it?" Uncle Jerome queried.

"No," I assured him. "It seems to me that the whole charade only makes sense is the hypothetical purpose is inverted."

"You're blithering again."

"No I'm not. Surely it only makes sense if the purpose of the exercise wasn't to recruit me to deliver a message in secret to Mercutio, but rather to draw Mercutio's attention—or, more specifically, Arlecchino's attention—to me."

"To you? So far as I can see, that makes far less sense. You don't have anything to do with this."

"No, I don't. If someone wanted to draw attention to me, it could only be in order to deflect it from someone else."

"It still doesn't make any sense."

"It might," I said, "if the person who supposedly has the Portals of Paradise and has brought them here to sell—or who is pretending to have them and has come here to work a bizarre confidence trick—is an Englishman…a Merchant Adventurer. Someone we met in Paris, perhaps—someone ostensibly making the Grand Tour."

"Who? You can't possibly mean Kenavan or Heckenfield."

"Why not? They're both here. You've seen them, and renewed your acquaintance with them. And if not one of them, someone who knows them."

"But potential buyers of the glass eyes, or the guild of *bravi*, couldn't possibly be stupid enough to be induced to think that *you* might have the magic eyes and that you've brought them to Venice to sell."

"Perhaps not," I said, "but perhaps the question is whether they might be induced to suspect *you*."

That suggestion actually gave Uncle Jerome pause for thought, as he considered his own self-cultivated reputation. Eventually, though, he said: "I don't believe it."

"Neither do I," I confessed. "But can you contrive a more satisfactory story?"

That gave him pause for thought too, but eventually forced the admission that he could not. Hopefully, however, he added: "Can you?"

"I'm a playwright," I said to him, only stretching the truth a little, because I had certainly written plays. "Of course I can. The problem is that all the other stories I can fit to the facts are more Gozzi than Goldoni, and perhaps too far beyond the bounds of possibility even for Gozzi to consider them plausible."

"Such as?" he queried.

"In a play," I said, "The Devil is only an actor playing the part… but within the story being told, he really is the Devil. In *Il Diavolo in Badgad*, the magical eyes are the Devil's work, whether or not he employed a glassmaker to undertake the actual process of manufacture—but that raises further questions, that the play only addressed obliquely. Why did the Devil make the magical eyes? How was he able to make them, if they do, in fact, offer access to a partial experience of Paradise, with which he supposedly has no truck?"

"I'm not following this at all," Uncle Jerome confessed.

"You didn't see *Il Diavolo in Bagdad*," I said, as if that were explanation enough. "In the play, the Devil has some kind of prior agreement with the characters standing in for the Berovieros, as well as one with the Mooress standing in for Zulietta Zellini, and it's the conflict between those two agreements that generates the confusion of the conclusion. The original version of the legend is simpler, but perhaps that's why it's so puzzling, why there appears to be a piece missing.

"If I were to write a play based on the legend—as I'll surely be tempted to do, now that I've been introduced to it—I'd take full advantage of the license to introduce the impossible and the fantastic. I'd provide an explanation of why the Devil enabled Pietro Beroviero to make the Portals of Paradise, and how he was able to contrive that peculiar miracle. I'd also provide an explanation of why the Devil was so upset when the eyes were stolen from Bartholomeo Collatino by one or both of the *bravi*, and exactly what vengeance he exacted upon them…and why he retained an interest in the eyes thereafter."

"What explanation?" Uncle Jerome enquired, dutifully.

"I don't know," I said, "because I haven't written the play yet, but I'd certainly provide one, for the sake of esthetic satisfaction. Because I'm not a Venetian, writing for a Venetian audience, I'd feel free to invent an authentic denouement, because I wouldn't feel that I had to maintain any reverence for the incompleteness of the original legend. There are doubtless many possibilities, most of which haven't yet crossed my mind yet, but there's one obvious point from which to start."

"Which is?"

"The beginning, of course: what happened when I stumbled over the Devil in the dark."

Uncle Jerome had even less idea of what I was talking about by now than when I'd started, and he was beginning to look more annoyed than bewildered.

"I gave him a drink of water," I said.

"So you said. So what?"

"It was an act of kindness, in response to his need."

"And?"

"And then he invited me to think about his existential situation. It was all play-acting, of course—just a game. But when I write my play about the Portals of Paradise, and I have a license to deal with the impossible, I'll take aboard the notion that occurred to me then, of the Devil being more to be pitied than feared, a Devil whose exile is an excessive reaction to the offense he gave: a Devil who appreciates an act of kindness, and feels a sense of obligation in consequence. And in my play, I could probably explain the Devil's generosity in creating the Portals of Paradise for Bartolomeo Collatino as a repayment for an act of kindness previously carried out in his regard by Pietro Beroviero—and a repayment that had particular significance to him because it was a gift of something that he had lost and could never hope to recover. And that, I could probably argue, in my reinterpretation of the legend, is why he was so angry with the thieves who stole the eyes from Bartolomeo, and why he has never lost interest in the fate of the separated eyes."

Uncle Jerome emptied the dregs from his glass in a very studied manner.

"So," he said, when he had swallowed them, and scowled slightly at the taste of the deposit, "if, as you put it so eloquently, we had a license to deal with the impossible, the fake Devil you tripped over might have been the real Devil disguised as a fake, for whom you performed a rare act of kindness, and who reciprocated by offering you protection in order that you could attend a performance of a play that drives men mad?"

"A playwright might interpret what had happened that way, if he were to make a drama out of my own adventure," I agreed. "But as a *philosophe*, I have no license for any such interpretation...even though, in a purely esthetic sense, it seems far more satisfactory than the commonsensical explanation that someone—Kenevan, Heckenfield, or some other bear-leader who has visited Venice before, perhaps several times, has had the crazy ambition of trying to exploit a local legend to bring off some kind of imbecilic confidence trick."

"I see what you mean," said Uncle Jerome, pensively. He was obviously still working the mechanism of his mind ardently, trying to think of a third story more satisfactory to him than either of those.

"As a matter of interest," he added, as we stood up, in order to make our way, at a leisurely walk, to the hotel where the Harringtons were staying. "How much do you think the Portals of Paradise might fetch at auction?"

"I can't even make a guess," I said. "It would depend, would it not, on how many blind men there are in Venice who have access to much larger fortunes than poor Mercutio—and how many inhabitants of this conspicuously Decadent city might be perversely willing to trade their sighted eyes for a glimpse of paradise."

"They wouldn't fetch a saucerful of spittle in Bristol," Uncle Jerome opined, speaking as a true son of Archibald Bowlands, "or thirty guineas in London…but in Venice, or Italy entire…like you, I can't even make a guess. There are a lot of crazy people in the world, and not all of them are poor."

IX

TEA WITH ADELAIDE

As a playwright, naturally, I had to be prepared to deal with the mythology of love, as it had been laboriously developed by countless playwrights, poets, story-tellers and legend-mongers before me: a mythology that included such hallowed notions as star-crossed lovers and love at first sight. As a *philosophe*, on the other hand, I was obliged to be skeptical of such fancies. Was it really plausible that merely seeing Adelaide Harrington at a distance, in Paris, and meeting her gaze less than half a dozen times, could have instilled a conviction in me that she was uniquely qualified to inspire true passion within me, let alone that the conviction in question might be mirrored in her mind?

Obviously, the philosophical answer to that question was no. It was not plausible that any such circumstance could really occur. It was not plausible, either, that Tristan could have loved Isolde as he was said to do, or that Romeo could have loved Juliet as Shakespeare claimed, and even less plausible that Isolde could have loved Tristan in return and Juliet Romeo. Such things did not happen in real life, for the simple reason that they could not. They were beyond the bounds of actual possibility, belonging purely to the realm of Romantic ideas, to the paradisal portion of the imagination.

I knew that—and yet, there was something in me that stubbornly insisted on refusing the philosophical answer, in remaining Romantic. Perhaps it was a symptom of my youth, or my poetic temperament, but there was no getting past it. One way or another, Adelaide Harrington had attracted my attention in Paris, and once she had attracted it, I had become blind to all other amorous temptations. It was not merely that Uncle Jerome's attempts to induce me to visit the world-famous brothels of Paris had induced an invincible repulsion in me, but that the possibility of any perfectly virtuous and admirably pretty young woman causing my head to turn in another direction had simply been cancelled out.

I really was in love with Adelaide, before I had even spoken to her. Implausible as it may be, it was a fact.

In Uncle Jerome's eyes, of course, I was a perfect fool, and my "infatuation" with "the chit" was simply something that I had to "get over" in order to return to the real world of cunning amorous flirtation and vulgar sexual indulgence. From Uncle Jerome's point of view, the invitation to tea that Adelaide had forced her guardian to issue was welcome not because it created a possibility for our mutual interest in one another to progress to a further stage of mutual adoration, but because it offered an opportunity for my ideas to be dragged back down to earth, for my illusions to be shattered and my ambitions to be dispelled or vulgarized, as appropriate.

In spite of that conflict of attitudes—and, indeed, because of it—Uncle Jerome accepted fully that his own role in the occasion was to distract the dragon and allow Adelaide and myself the maximum opportunity to inspect one another at close range and to explore, through polite conversation, the actual extent of our common interests, opinions and attitudes. I must admit that in that regard, he was positively heroic. I don't say that he would have gone so far as to attempt to seduce the maiden aunt and do everything in his power to persuade her to fall in love with him, but he was certainly prepared to be as charming as humanly possible, and to put on a show of finding her ideas and interests perfectly fascinating.

The tea was served from a Russian samovar, or perhaps a Turkish semaver, and had a strength and savor to match, so the imitation of an English tea party was far from perfect, but that did not matter in the least. We could have been drinking tar for all I cared.

The opening gambit of our conversation was, of course, already set out for us. We were there, ostensibly, to talk about out mutual interest in the theater, and where could we possibly begin, except with *Il Diavolo in Badgad*, as a specimen of the Gozzi method and influence?

Politeness demanded that I should seek her impressions first, and I was glad of the opportunity to hear her voice expound at length. It was the most beautiful voice in all the world, although I know that you can't believe me when I say so. After all, though, you weren't there; I was.

"I confess," she said, "that I didn't understand it at all. My Italian is weak by comparison with my French, and the Venetian dialect is even more difficult to follow than mainland Italian. I'm fascinated by Gozzi's use of folktales, and I loved the French adaptation of *Turandot* that I saw in Paris, but the material in yesterday's play was so strange that I couldn't even begin to grasp it. If you could explain it to me, Mr. Bowlands, I'd be exceedingly grateful to you."

The voice in which that charming request was made was, as I say, wonderfully musical—and the way that she fluttered her eyelashes as she issued her delicate prompt sent a thrill through my entire body.

She was, of course, sincere; she really was in quest of an explanation of the play, but asking me for an explanation was also a means to an end. She wanted to hear me speak at length, in order to measure my intellect and personality. She really was interested in me. Perhaps it was only because of my golden hair and angelic face that she had noticed me to begin with, and perhaps the illusion created by that appearance might have been shattered at any moment, but the simple fact was that she was at least prepared to entertain the possibility of liking me.

And I did my very best to rise to the challenge and to make the very most of the opportunity, I told her the story of Bartolomeo Collatino and Caterina di Mastropietro, and the Portals of Paradise, as Mercutio had told it to me, and I explained how the actors playing the pirate and the Devil had modified and complicated the elements of that legend in making a new play of it. She seemed to follow the argument more accurately than Uncle Jerome had, or at least she pretended to do so. She seemed to be doing her utmost to think of intelligent questions.

"And all this happened only thirty-nine years ago?" she queried, with reference to the story of Bartolomeo Collatino. "It is, therefore, more history than folklore?"

"It's certainly a legend of recent formation," I agreed. "We've been fortunate enough to see an early phase of the transition from legend to literature, and witness that process in action."

"But the actors felt obliged to change the location of the drama, and to alter the nature of the characters, because some of the people featured in the anecdote must still be alive?"

"Some of them might be," I agreed. "But they must be very old, if so."

"Not so very old," she suggested. "If Caterina and Zulietta were only twenty when they married, or even younger, as they might well have been, they would probably be sixty now, or thereabouts. In those days, as now, men frequently married women much younger than themselves, but even if all the men who figured in the story are dead, the two leading ladies might well be respectable dowagers eking out their widowhood—and doubtless still hating one another with an intense fervor."

I judged from that observation that Adelaide had a sense of the dramatic, but also that she had an acute intelligence; I had not thought of the matter in those precise terms. Automatically, I immediately began to reexamine my remembered impressions of the woman who had summoned me to Murano. I had initially wanted to think of her as young, and the idea that she might be the window Senedese, who was said to be still young, had encouraged that desire—but I had soon decided, on the basis of our interaction, that she was akin to the mature Parisiennes who had been drawn to me by a curious combination of maternal and lustful feelings. Surely it was more than merely possible that her interest in the Portals of Paradise went back to the very beginning of the story?

According to the authors of *Il Diavolo in Bagdad*, I remembered, the Mooress standing in for Zulietta Zellini had been specifically condemned by the Devil to search for the four scattered eyes and to reunite them if she could. Eduardo Lucca had claimed that his co-author had access to more information that the standard version of the legend. What, I wondered, did he think he knew, and how reliable was his conviction? Zulietta, if what Lucca had told me could be trusted, had had a bravo for a cicisbeo, and had called on the services of another, then presumably a friend but later…

I shelved the train of thought firmly, however. For the time being, I had to focus all my attention on Adelaide.

"The transfiguration of the story into a pastiche of Galland is interesting in itself as an example of the literary adaptation of legendary materials," I observed, looking into her lovely eyes and drinking in their apparent fascination with what I was saying, "especially the syncretic combination of elements from different sources, which allows the juxtaposition of the character of the peri and with that of the Devil."

She didn't blink at the use of the word "syncretic"—either she was a true intellectual or a good actress.

"But that process of combination and mixing of various elements began long ago," she said, "in the work of Shakespeare and his contemporaries. If you are ambitious to be a playwright in England and to import something of the spirit of Carlo Gozzi into your own work, Mr. Bowlands, you are already heir to a folklore that has various layers: Celtic, Saxon and Norman, as well as the legacy of the Greek and Latin drama. What comedies you might be able to make, if you can break the chains of English tradition after the fashion of Signor Gozzi in Italy! That process has hardly begun even in Paris, although Monsieur Voltaire and his colleagues have certainly begun to point the way, but in London…imagine what might be done there with an adaptation of *Il Diavolo in Bagdad*? You would have to devise a neater ending, though. Simply scattering the four magical eyes is anti-climactic, don't you think?"

"Absolutely," I agreed.

"Nor could I understand exactly what the other pair of glass eyes was supposed to do, in magical terms. What, after all, in involved in being able to see djinn—demons or angels in our terminology—and precisely what advantage does it confer? Can they grant wishes, like the djinn in the Arabian Nights? That notion needs more work if it is to play a proper role in the narrative."

"You think like a playwright yourself, Miss Harrington," I said. "Have you written dramas of your own?"

She blushed; I had hit the nail on the head. "Technically," she hedged, "although I am certainly Miss Harrington, in present company it would be more conventional to address me as Miss Adelaide, in order to avoid confusion with my aunt, Miss Harrington…although personally, I would prefer a simple Adelaide, if I might be permitted to address you as Gabriel?"

"Of course," I said, "I would be delighted."

"Then I shall," she declared. "As for being a writer myself, London is not so far advanced as Paris in that regard. Even in Paris, writers like Madame Riccoboni, Mademoiselle Falque and Olympe de Gouges remain exceptional, and are not taken as seriously as they deserve. Yes, I would love to write plays, or perhaps novels, but you can have no idea of the difficulties facing a woman of such ambition, even within her own family." She glanced at her aunt, who seemed to be discussing politics with Uncle Jerome, with a warmth that suggested that he might have temporarily set aside his Whiggish views and suppressed his enthusiasm for the ideas of Charles James Fox.

"You have my sympathies," I assured her. "My own difficulties as a literary man in a family of cotton traders must be trivial by comparison."

"My aunt is under the impression that the cotton trade and the slave trade are one and the same," Adelaide observed. "Not that she's a fervent abolitionist, mind, but she considers all trade as beneath the dignity of what she calls *true gentlemen*."

"The Bowlands have never been involved in the slave trade," I told her, "and at the risk of causing offense, I am a fervent abolitionist. Such fortune as I might one day inherit has, however, certainly been made in commerce, and I must confess that I have no entitlement to be considered a *true gentleman* in the sense that Miss Harrington interprets the phrase."

I was being ridiculously pedantic of course, for an angelic adolescent, but Adelaide did not seem to mind in the least—indeed, she seemed to be relishing my performance.

"Nonsense," she retorted, as I had hoped that she would. "A *true* gentleman is defined by his character, not by the source of his income.

What credit can possibly be due to us by virtue of the fact that one or other of our ancestors obtained the title to land by the gift of some king? Your family, by contrast, has earned its money by honest effort."

Some people might have considered the attribution of the success of the Bowlands to honest effort rather than the vagaries of the marketplace a generous assessment—including, I suspected, Miss Harrington—but I was very grateful for Adelaide's choice of that interpretation. I was exceedingly grateful, too, for the fraction of the conversation that cannot be reproduced in the mere reportage of words: the smiles and associated changes of expression, the generosity of her gaze, which had not wavered in close confrontation any more than my admiration for her.

As time went by, and we found more polite questions to ask of one another, and more polite answers to proffer in return, that wordless fraction became increasingly important, and its warmth brought my heart slowly to the boil, far more effectively than anything that was actually said. I still insist that I had been in love before I even entered the room, but I was certainly even more deeply and irrevocably in love by the time that Miss Harrington's severe notion of etiquette demanded that my uncle and I leave.

Now that Adelaide and I had been properly introduced, there was no barrier to my requesting permission to see her again, and to issue as many future requests of that kind as circumstances might permit, so my confidence that my blossoming love had a future was immense. I was walking on air, as the cliché has it, or perhaps even dancing.

I did not need any glass baubles to give me the conviction that, from that moment on, there was an element of paradise in my existence, in which I might be able to dwell forever.

There were several stages of the Grand Tour yet to go, and I knew that it would only require a trivial comparison of itineraries to make sure that Adelaide and I met again after leaving Venice, probably in Florence, surely in Rome, and perhaps in Naples too. Perhaps, I thought, it would even be possible to co-ordinate our eventual return to England so as to travel on the same ship. Once we were back in England, of course, the distance between Bristol and Kent might prove problematic, but not in any fashion that could not be overcome, with true determination on my part and hers—and by the time that Miss Harrington expelled us from that initial tea party, I no longer had the slightest doubt that there was a steely determination on both sides of the problematic equation.

Once we were back in the multicolored crowd—which no longer seemed to be as dispirited and false as it had on the previous days—and I was able to breathe easily again, I offered Uncle Jerome my fulsome thanks.

"Actually," he said, "it wasn't that bad. She's not an unpleasant woman, but she does feel a powerful sense of responsibility to protect her brother's daughter, perhaps inevitably as she has none of her own. I couldn't pry, of course, so I wasn't able to discover how she came to be left on the shelf, but I got the impression that it wasn't by choice. I suspect that she had to care for her parents, and perhaps her brother too, during much of the interval in which she could have been courted conventionally, and probably was."

"She doesn't seem so very old," I commented.

"No, she's well-preserved—partly, no doubt, because she never had children—but if my judgment can be trusted, she's over fifty. It didn't stop her from looking at poor Adelaide with a hint of jealousy in her eye, though—mixed feelings there, I suspect. If you're careful to pay her the occasional compliment and smile at her now again again, you can probably win her over…if you still want to."

"Oh yes," I assured him.

"It went well, then? No disillusionment?"

"Very well indeed, and not a trace."

"Good luck to you, then, I'll do what I can to maintain friendly relations. Don't rush it, though. Remember that there are two sets of parents who'll have to be straightened out, if anything is to come of it…and don't be too disappointed if it fizzles out before we even get to Rome."

"It won't," I told him, firmly.

We parted then, as I had to go to the theater.

As a complete change of pace, I was sampling a tragedy by the Milanese dramatist Alessandro Verri, the brother of one of the leading philosophers of the Italian Enlightenment and the translator of Shakespeare's tragedies into Italian. It was an anomalous inclusion in the calendar of the Carnival of Venice, but I was glad to find it in performance there two days before Ash Wednesday. It proved easier to follow than any of the comedies I had seen, partly because of its solemnity and partly because it was unaffected by improvisations in Venetian dialect.

When I returned to the hotel after the performance, Uncle Jerome was not there, doubtless enjoying himself somewhere in the city, and I did not attempt to wait for his return before going to bed. I had had an emotional day, which had buoyed up my spirits considerably, even in the throes of Verri's tragedy, and I had finally been deflected somewhat from my incessant mental wrangling with the enigma of the artificial Portals of Paradise.

I had not forgotten, however, that the following day was Shrove

Tuesday, when *Il Re giallo* was due to be performed at the Teatro Festim, and my dreams were strangely confused. Adelaide featured within them along with the Devil and the dark lady, in a strange amalgam that seemed all the more ominous because it was entangling two entirely separate threads of my existence.

While I had been discussing *Il Diavolo in Badgad* with Adelaide the puzzle of the Portals of Paradise had been reduced to an accessory of my attempt to impress her, and my actual involvement in the present manifestation of the affair, carefully umentioned, had seemed suddenly remote. In my dreams, however, the affair no longer seemed remote, but too close for comfort, and it was not the elder Miss Harrington that I imagined casting jealous glances at me as I tried to impress Adelaide but the dark lady, who had now been reconfigured in my imagination as someone far older than I had initially envisaged her, and someone with a dark secret: specifically, I was leaning toward the hypothesis that she was Zulietta Zellini, similarly confused in my present imagination with a Moorish witch and dark minion of the Devil.

But they were, after all, only dreams, and when I woke up the following morning, they faded away almost completely, only leaving a few forceful but sparse images and some fugitive impressions of discomfort and danger.

X

UNCLE JEROME'S DISAPPEARANCE

I was not unduly surprised, when I woke up, to discover that Uncle Jerome had not come back all night. It was by no means the first time it had happened, and he had very rarely given me any advance warning of his intention, simply because he had often had no such intention when he set forth. Not was it always his exploration of the brothels of Europe that kept him away; when he went out drinking with his fellow bear-leaders, especially the seasoned traveler Lord Kenavan and the kindred spirit Mr. Heckenfield, such excursions often extended until one or more of them had passed out.

My first thought was that the success of my meeting with Adelaide and the relative ease of his conversation with the elder Miss Harrington might have instilled a yearning for female company in him, prompting him to go out whoring. On reflection, however, it also seemed possible that my rather fanciful story, in which someone might be attempting to deflect attention from themselves by drawing attention to him as a possible custodian of one or more of the Portals of Paradise, in the course of which Kenavan and Heckenfield had been named, might have sent him forth on an expedition of a different kind, in the attempt to reassure himself that it was nonsense, or at least determine whether it was possible.

As the morning wore on, however, the former hypothesis gradually seemed less likely, and the latter, albeit improbably, more ominous. I had not been serious, of course, in suggesting that I might have been recruited as a clandestine messenger in order to create the suspicion that Uncle Jerome might have been the sender of the message, and thus implicated in the prospective auction of the glass eyes. I had produced the account in the spirit of a dramatist, just as I had produced the alternative supernatural hypothesis, and like Uncle Jerome, I had immediately begun casting around for a third alternative explanation that would seem more plausible than either. I had not come up with any such hypothesis in the interim, however, and I suspected that Uncle Jerome could not have done any better—in which case, he might have begun to find the hypothesis that I had voiced worthy of investigation.

If he had, I thought, what if it had turned out to be true? What if his attempt to investigate the possibility that Kenavan, Heckenfield, or one of their mutual acquaintances, had brought one or more of Pietro Beroviero's glass eyes to Venice had called further attention to himself, and further suspicion? What if the guild of *bravi* had become involved?

Even in the unlikely event that that might be true, however, what could I possibly do about it? What could I possibly do about it, in any case? To report to the authorities that a Tourist had not returned to his hotel all night after the eve of Shrove Tuesday would only generate knowing laughter, not alarm. Even if he failed to come back the following night as well, the final night of the Carnival, who would construe that as evidence of foul play, especially if I mentioned anything at all about the reasons for my suspicions. The Portals of Paradise? The guild of *bravi*? The knowing smiles would grow into uproarious laughter. There was no possibility of registering the disappearance with the authorities until Thursday, at the earliest—and even then, the absentee was a Tourist. Who would be surprised? Who would care?

The only thing capable of changing that attitude, I knew, would be the discovery of a dead body—by which time, obviously, it would be far too late.

At noon, a sealed note was brought up to my room from the hotel office, addressed to me. I opened it half-expecting to find a ransom note, and then cursed myself for my folly. The note was from Adelaide, thanking me for accepting her invitation of the previous day and expressing the hope that we might meet again soon. I realized immediately that I should have been the one writing to thank her and her aunt, and cursed Uncle Jerome for not having reminded me of that before I set off for Verri's tragedy.

I repaired the omission instantly, and hurried down to the office to ask the clerk on duty to find a messenger to make the delivery. While I was still there, after having handed the missive to the summoned commissionnaire, another package arrived at the hotel, addressed to me. That one was bulky, though not very heavy, and it was wrapped in stout paper, bound with string and very carefully sealed.

I took the package up to my room, wondering what it could possibly contain, and then took several minutes severing various pieces of string with a pen-knife, in order to break through the complex binding. In the end, though, I reached the contents, and displayed them, with considerable wonderment and not a little alarm.

The package contained a hooded costume, complete with mask, simple enough in design but dramatic in its coloration. The principal garment was a vast and luxurious satin robe with an equally capacious hood, colored brilliantly yellow. There was a shirt too, and a sturdy cummerbund, and neatly-woven hose, all in the same brilliant yellow, even though they would hardly show beneath the robe. The accompanying mask was neither a porcelain mould of a face nor a conventional *bauta*; it was shaped to cover the forehead, the eyes and the bridge of the nose—save for two unusually discreet eye-holes—but the opaque fabric then gave way to a fringe such as one sees at the bottom of an ornamental curtain, whose silken threads hung down over the mouth and chin.

It was not until I had picked the various pieces of costume that I saw that there was a wand too, lurking at the bottom of the bundle. I picked it up and studied it carefully. The shaft was yellow, but the head was painted as well as shaped to resemble the flames of a torch. The weight of the device seemed all wrong until I pulled the head experimentally, at which point a gleaming blade came free from its sheath. The wand was a swordstick, although the blade was not long enough to qualify as a foil; it was more like an assassin's dagger.

There was also a note, carefully folded into the satin robe. It read:

Gabriel.

    For tonight's performance, if you are sufficiently courageous. If you decide to wear it, cover it with a cloak until you arrive in the box, and then display it with pride. Have no fear: you have my promise that no harm will come to you, that you shall hear the whole story, and that you have every chance of witnessing its denouement.

                                  L.

Apparently, Lucifer wanted me to play the part of the King in Yellow during the performance of *Il Re giallo*.

There was, however, a world of uncertainty hidden beneath the word *apparently*. Could I be sure that the note had been sent by the same individual that had invited me to the performance and given me the mysterious pass? Even if I accepted that as true, who was that individual, really? The Devil? An actor from Eduardo Lucca's troupe? A soldier of fortune whose normal role was that of bear-leader? And whichever of those equally ludicrous possibilities turned out to be true, if any of them did, what on earth could be the purpose of that invitation to dress up as a demonic incarnation of menace capable of driving men mad?

There was one further possibility that occurred to me, which was that the note and the costume had been sent by Uncle Jerome, that he had been behind the key elements of the affair all along—but I set that firmly aside, not because I thought Uncle Jerome incapable of playing a bizarre practical joke on me, but because he simply did not have the imagination required to invent the one in question.

Who, then, had sent me that dubious gift? And why?

That question too I set aside, simply because it seemed insoluble for the moment. The question I could not set aside, however—at least, not for long—was the question of what I was going to do. Was I really going to go along with the comedy? Was I really going to dress as the King in Yellow for a supposed performance of the accursed play? Was I even going to risk going to Giudecca and making my way to the Teatro Festim?

I had, of course, already decided to go, to accept the Devil's invitation at least to the extent of watching the forbidden play and whatever negotiations might follow. Why, then, should I not go all the way? If I had, in fact, agreed to play the Devil's comedy, should I not accept the whole of my role, whether I knew the dramatic purpose of my costume or not? Was I not, in fact, sufficiently courageous?

You have to remember that I was a man in love, a man dancing on air, a man who had glimpsed paradise. Yes, I was sufficiently courageous. I was ready to fight dragons, giants, windmills, or whatever fate had in store for me.

And after all, what harm could it do? I would not, in fact, *be* the King in Yellow. I would not be driving anyone mad merely by virtue of my presence. In all probability, I would not be the only person who would come to the theater in such a costume—not to mention that the actor appointed to play the role on the stage would have to wear one. No one would actually mistake me for the King in Yellow, would they? And even if someone did, what would their reaction be? They would hardly attack me in consequence.

I looked at the note again, paying particular attention to the final sentence.

What could the promise that no harm would come to me actually be worth, I wondered, whether it came from the Devil himself or some bizarre impostor? On the other hand, who could actually want to harm me, and why? As for the second and third element of the promise…well, what possible confidence could I have in those, whether the assurances came from the Devil or not? Did he know the whole story? Did anyone? And what denouement could it possibly have, in the context of whatever haggling or madness followed the climax of the improvised play?

On the other hand, would not any attempt to complete the story be worth hearing and seeing, as a matter of purely esthetic satisfaction? I certainly did not feel confident, as yet, of making one up myself that would come remotely close to plausibility or roundness, and whatever I heard or saw at the Teatro Festim would be welcome as a supplement to what I had heard and seen already.

I wished that Uncle Jerome was there, so that I could at least ask his advice, even if I then decided to ignore it completely. Already, however, I had a strong conviction that Uncle Jerome was not going to return before the time came to set off for Guidecca. I no longer had any doubt that someone intended me to go to the performance alone, as the Devil had instructed me to do.

Oddly enough, though, I was not afraid that Uncle Jerome might have been murdered. The hand and mind behind the comedy were surely far less brutal than that, and had a far finer sense of esthetics. I had every confidence that I would see Uncle Jerome alive and well on Ash Wednesday…assuming that I survived until then myself.

But why should I not survive, since I had the guarantee of the Devil's protection?

I sat down on the bed beside the costume and stared at it for a while. I did not have to try it on to see whether it fit. It was sufficiently loose fitting to fit almost anyone.

Why me? I thought, finally reducing all the questions to one.

That was a good question. Why, of all the people here to gawp at the Carnival of Venice, had I been selected to play the King in Yellow? That must surely have been the intention all along, I now thought, the other phases of the adventure being mere prelude. When the Devil had handed me my tempting invitation, he had already planned to send me the yellow costume.

But *why?* Why *me?*

The chronology of the adventure suggested that if the Devil had actually been lying in wait for me, it could only be because he knew, somehow, about the invitation to the rendezvous that the dark lady had sent me. But there again, why me? It had not, as I first imagined, been the mere coincidence of our standing on opposite balconies. She was not the widow Senedes; the balcony on which she had been standing was not her apartment, and she was probably not the same dark lady that I had met in Murano, but a mere stand-in. She was nevertheless there in anticipation of my being there, in order to see me, and to be seen by me. But why?

The story had started, I now knew for sure, in Paris. It was there what I had first been marked down for my role in the adventure. By whom? By the Devil? No, it was not yet time to invoke that all-purpose argumentative response. By Eduardo Lucca, or the manager of his troupe, or one of his fellow actors? Possibly. Or by one of Uncle Jerome's fellow bear-leaders? That was possible too.

But in either case, or neither, who was the dark lady? Was she one of the matrons who had looked at me with nostalgic lust while telling her rosary beds? Conceivably—but that didn't answer the question of who she might really be, in terms of her involvement with the Portals of Paradise. In my dreams, I had seized the hypothesis that she was Zulietta Zellini, who had been recast as a witch by Lucca and his co-author, but now I was awake, I had lost the sense of conviction that dreams sometimes have. If she was not Zulietta Zelini, however, who else could she be, if she really were one of the characters in the original story, but Caterina di Mastropietro, who had been recast as a Gallandesque peri by the same playmakers?

Time and time again, I kept coming back to Lucca, the loquacious actor. The whole affair was saturated with theatricality; no matter how serious some of the players might be, the whole was a fantastic comedy, and Eduardo Lucca was, like me, an aspirant playwright, eager to impress. He had played Pierrot and a pirate with equal facility; could he not have played the Devil too, in a costume borrowed from his fellow and collaborator? Or might he, too, be simply an instrument, and the man I had met in the dark back-street the man who normally wore the costume, another pretender to the metaphorical throne that Carlo Gozzi seemed to have left vacant, in spite of still being very much alive?

There was, I knew, only one way to find out. There was only one way that I was ever going to obtain any clarification, if any clarification could, in fact, be obtained.

And having come to that conclusion, with my decision firmly made, I left the costume on the bed and went downstairs and out into the street to take a final stroll through the final magnificence of the Carnival of Venice.

All the vivacity had returned to it now, and the animation no longer seemed forced. The Carnival was in full swing, and the apparatus of the Commedia was everywhere. There were Arlecchinos by the hundred, Pierrots by the dozen, Columbinas by the score, Capitan Spaventas swaggering, Brighellas sidling and Pantalones strutting. And everywhere there were *larvae*, outnumbering *bautas*, *morettas* and *medico della pestes* by a factor of ten.

There were Devils too, of course, and pirates, and peri princesses, but they were fugitive figures, seemingly lost in the great tide. The quintessence of the Carnival was the Commedia, and everything else was mere froth and jetsam. Even the Tourists, whether young men like my-self or bear-leaders like Uncle Jerome, had either donned costumes bor-rowed from the commedia or relegated themselves to the peripheral ob-scurity where I was confined in my black costume and my white mask.

Yes, it was Decadent; yes, it was perverse—but it was also mag-nificent, now that it had recovered its verve and brio. If it was a mani-festation of twilight, it was one of those last bright beams that the sun sometimes throws off as a final flourish, as if casually and contemptu-ously, before disappearing behind the horizon and leaving only a legacy of dying light.

No one—absolutely no one—was costumed as the King in Yellow.

The site on the Piazza where Mercutio the Cheiromancer had pitched his tent was vacant. He and his *bravo* Arlecchino had packed up and gone, although other fortune-tellers seemed to be busier than on any previous day. I wasn't tempted—and not because Mercutio had already given me the vague indications that he had pretended to read in my hand.

I ate a hasty meal before returning to the hotel, and then I donned my costume. I tucked up the hem in order to be able to stride freely, and I left the hood down in order that a black cloak could cover it com-pletely. I stowed the wand inside the cloak, and went to the door of the room…before hesitating, and turning back.

The cummerbund was devoid of loops, but it fitted tightly enough to give it the resilience to support the scabbard of my rapier with the aid of a hook. The sheath was not yellow, and nor was the weapon's hand-guard but I did not think that the slight clash of colors would detract too deleteriously from the intended image, and I felt a good deal more secure knowing that I had the familiar weapon by my side than I would have done with only the short blade hidden in the wand.

Even though it was the Eve of Lent, I had no difficult finding a boat-man to ferry me to Guidecca. He barely cast a glance at the *volto* that was covering my yellow mask in a distinctly awkward fashion, having no reason to waste wonderment on the fact that a crazy tourists was stacking masks one atop another.

Once on the island, I had no difficulty locating the street on which the Teatro Festim was located. The building was dark externally, but its doors were guarded by a number of men costumed in what I immedi-ately recognized as the old uniform of the guild of *bravi*, completed by a black volto. Perhaps it was merely a costume, and perhaps not. I showed the sheet from my notebook on which the Devil had scribbled, however, and was instantly admitted. Evidently, the strange language, if it was a language, was recognizable to the imitation *bravi*.

The most problematic part of the entire journey might have been locating the box that had been allotted to me, but once the doorman had admitted me he summoned an usher similarly clad in a uniform and a black *volto*, and the latter led me silently upstairs and into what appeared to me to be the second box along from the proscenium. It contained two seats, and I took the one nearer to the stage.

Then I took off my cloak and my white *volto*, exposing the yellow robe and mask, pulled the yellow hood over my head, and leaned forward, placing my elbows on the cushioned rim of the box.

XI

IL RE GIALLO

The theater was a little larger than I had expected, and a good deal more ornate. As Eduardo Lucca had said, the interior had been recently and elaborately remodeled, but showed no sign of having been used previously for its intended purpose. As in all the newly-redesigned theatres of Venice, the architects had adopted modern conventions, so the stage was raised, surrounded in front by a proscenium arch and cloaked by a huge curtain, but, as in many other theaters of similar design, there was no gallery. There was space for four boxes to either side, although, obviously, I could only see into the interior of those opposite, none of which were occupied at the moment when I first sat down. The chairs and sofas on the floor below were arranged in twelve rows, with a distinctly crooked aisle in the middle.

I had arrived punctually, as a good Englishman should, and had expected the floor to be three-quarters empty, just as the boxes opposite were, because Venetians are as habitually late as the Portuguese, but I saw that I had mistaken the eagerness of the audience below. Almost every seat was already taken.

The crowd was as brightly-clad as any I had seen on any of my previous theatrical excursions, but it was much quieter. I thought that I had grown used to the irony of seeing more costumes in the audience than on stage—the players in previous performances I had attended had gone to such great pains to make the most of it that their asides had become distinctly tedious—but as soon as I set eyes on this crowd I realized that there were depths of comedic confusion that had yet to be tapped.

One of the side-effects of Goldoni and Gozzi's loosening of the old conventions of the *comedia dell'arte* on stage had been a parallel loosening of the styling of conventional costumes. One result of that fluidity was that all the people who donned the traditional costumes, whether as players on a stage or participants in the Carnival of the streets, had considerable opportunity to stamp their own personalities upon their impostures. Thus, one might see three Pierrots sitting in a row in a theater audience, or two Scaramucchias engaged in earnest conversation, and yet be able to see that they were different as well as similar: acting, as it were, in different plays, or at least in different versions of the same play. Improvisation was evident everywhere that I had visited in the previous three days, carefully paraded for the knowing eye.

That improvisation and individualization seemed, however, to be missing from the crowd assembled in the theatre to which I had come as a highly distinctive fantasy in yellow, where the vast majority of costumes seemed to be rigidly conventional, and many seemed to be cut from identical templates. I counted no less than eight patchwork Arlecchinos in the audience, five crow-like Scaramucchias and four voluminously-caped Capitan Spaventas, but each one was indistinguishable from the others of his type. All their costumes were standardized.

I quickly concluded that they were actually striving for anonymity, deliberately cultivating confusion, hiding among others of their assumed ilk. Then I realized, however, that if that were really the case, they were only courting that confusion with respect to a fraction of the people around them, because the rest could not see them at all.

The simple fact was that perhaps as many as one in three of the men gathered on the floor of the auditorium were sightless. There were some ninety men there, and I estimated, once I had made a careful survey, that as many as thirty of them were probably blind. I could not see the eyes—or lack of eyes—behind the masks they wore, but I could see by the manner of their conversation and their lack of visual curiosity that the people around them might as well have been clad in monkish robes or workmen's blouses. More than half of the sighted majority, I guessed, must be the servants of the blind men, whose task was to guide them, but there seemed to me to be a remainder there on their own behalf. *Bravi? Merchant adventurers?* Possibly—but how could I tell?

Had there ever been such an audience as that in any theater in the world? I think not. In fact, I was certain of it, and still am. I tried to identify the particular Arlecchino who had been stationed outside the tent of Mercutio the Cheiromancer, and Mercutio himself, but he too must have donned a costume and a secretive mask in order to disappear from view in the crowd.

Perhaps it is unsurprising, given the constitution of the audience, that the appearance of an individual costumed as the King in Yellow did not attract as much attention as I had naively anticipated, but even after I had realized that so many of the "spectators" were blind, the lack of reaction among the rest seemed odd. Many, if not all of the sighted men in the crowd must have noticed my arrival almost immediately, but if they turned to look in my direction they did it furtively and swiftly, and then looked away again, as if determined not to react.

Had they expected to see the costume or were they simply determined not to react to anything unusual? I could not tell.

The empty boxes opposite did not remain empty for long. Two figures soon moved into the one nearest to the stage; the single chair therein was taken by a woman, whose gaudy gown was sown with a thousand glass beads, while her companion—a man costumed as Scaramucchia—stood behind her. She was wearing a moretta, but her hood was down and her exposed hair was not the same jet black as that of the dark lady who had summoned me to the mysterious rendezvous.

A lone man occupied the second box; his costume was black as a Scaramucchia, save for white shirt-sleeves, but it was cut in a very severe fashion, fashioned from leather and linen rather than silks. His face was covered by a black *bauta*.

The third box had two seats, and again, one of them was occupied by a woman, this one clad in black with her hood up, covering her hair. She could have been the dark lady I had met on Murano, but it was impossible to be sure. She was accompanied by a Capitan Spaventa, indistinguishable from those on the floor.

The fourth box, like the second, was occupied by a lone man, this time costumed as Pierrot—one of four individuals in the audience to have chosen that guise, although there might conceivably have been another in one of the boxes on my side.

I had heard someone enter the box on my right—the one further away from the stage than my own, but if anyone had come into the one to the left of mine he or she had done so silently. I had no clue as to what might be happening in the fourth. In any case, my attention was primarily focused on the second seat in my own box. Who, I wondered, was going to occupy that one, and in what disguise?

It was still empty when lights in the auditorium went down and the curtain slowly rose, but almost immediately thereafter, the door opened and a man slipped in. He was clad entirely in black, with a black hood over his head, covering the entire pate, somewhat reminiscent of a medieval executioner. As I turned to stare at him, trying to find some indication in his stature and build of who he might be, he leaned close to my hood and whispered:

"Thank you, my young friend. I do not think you will regret your courage."

His voice, I thought, was definitely that of the Devil over whom I had stumbled in the alleyway in Santa Croce. He took the seat to my right, but he did not lean forward in order to obtain a better angle from which to view the stage. Indeed, if anything, he leaned back, into the shadows of the box, disappearing into darkness until the curtain reached the full extent of its slow rise.

At that point, he placed his ungloved left hand negligently upon the cushioned rail, with the fingers splayed. There was no doubt in my mind that the gesture was quite deliberate, and that its purpose was to show me that the ring-finger was entirely missing, having apparently been surgically severed at the base.

My companion either was, or at least wanted me to believe that he might be, Leandro di Mastropietro. But how could I possibly have guessed that the initial attached to the note accompanying my costume might have stood for Leandro and not for Lucifer? And how could I be sure, even with the aid of the visual evidence that he had just provided, that it did?

Abruptly, as you will readily understand, my entire perspective shifted, and I glimpsed the whole situation, and the whole comedy, in yet another different light—but it was only a glimpse; I did not have time to react, or even to rethink, because the play had begun, and the performance of what was at least pretending to be *Il Re giallo* was under way.

I turned my head reflexively, away from the hand with the missing finger and toward the stage. Unlike my companion, I did lean further forward in order to obtain a view, and succeeded—but I also obtained a view of the cushioned rail of the box to the left of my own, the one nearest the stage. That one too had been suddenly occupied, and there too, a male hand was negligently resting on the rail, the fingers dangling over the edge.

None of the fingers was missing, but the ring-finger caught and trapped my attention nevertheless because of the gold ring upon it, which seemed a little too tight for the finger that bore it, set with a rose-ate stone shaped like a heart. I noticed, too, that the skin on the back of the hand was smooth and youthful—and that the color and cloth of the sleeve from which the hand extended was exactly the same shade of yellow as my own costume.

I inferred that the hand was being dangled deliberately to show off the ring, just as my companion's hand had been placed where I was in order to display the missing ring-finger, from which that same ring had been stolen. But to whom were the two messages directed. To me? It seemed more likely that they were reciprocal. But if so, why was I there at all?

I did not doubt for an instant that the man in the box next to mine had to be wearing a costume identical to mine and carrying an identical wand. I immediately jumped to the conclusion that I was dressed as I was in order to create confusion as to which of us was the "real" King in Yellow.

Perhaps I would have stammered a question, but my companion's hand moved then, so that its four fingers descended lightly upon my shoulder.

"Watch the comedy, my friend," the Devil's voice advised. "You will find it amusing, I hope. During the entr'acte, if there is time, I will tell you another story."

So I held my tongue and watched, and did indeed find the comedy, if not exactly amusing, perfectly fascinating.

The version of *Il Re giallo* improvised for the Festim was yet anther version of the story of the Portals of Paradise. Given that the legend of the play dated back centuries before the events of the Venetian legend, it obviously had no possible claim to be "authentic" in any straightforward sense, but I knew that there had to be a reason for the borrowing of the title, and that it could not simply be a mere matter of false advertising.

This time, there was no displacement of the story to an Arabian Nights setting, and no substitution of names. The setting was a version of Venice, and the characters were named as they were in the version of the legend that Mercutio the Cheiromancr had summarized for me—except that this Venice was a magical one in which powerful families with affiliations to different fallen angels were locked in a continual rivalry that occasionally threatened to explode into murderous violence.

Such explosions were, however, routinely controlled and suppressed by the diplomacy of the Republic and its representative: not, in this fictitious Venice, the red-clad Doge, but the King in Yellow, the greatest of all the Venetian magicians, who employed various magical compensations as well as negotiating diplomatic compromises in order to maintain equilibrium in the never-ending conflict of family ambitions and resentments.

Negotiated marriages between adversarial factions were a routine means of symbolizing treaties between rival families, but sometimes, marriages between members of rival families occurred spontaneously, as a result of love matches, and one such love-match—apparently, at least—had prompted Leandro di Mastropieto to marry Caterina Beroviero, in the face of stern opposition by their kin, focused in Leandro's case in the disapproval of his sister Zulietta and in Caterina's by that of her father Pietro.

Leandro and Zulietta's husband, Andrea Zellini, were both young members of the Major Council of the fictitious Venice, constantly engaged in sometimes-violent political struggles involving elections to the Council of Ten and the appointment of the Supreme Inquisitors. Both men attached bodyguards to their wives: older members of the guild of *bravi*, with the special mission to protect the individuals committed to their care. Zulietta's bodyguard was Maurizio Scamozzi and Caterina's was Bartolomeo Collatino.

In this version of the story, Zulietta had attempted to seduce Leandro in order to break his marriage with Caterina, but had failed, even with the aid of amatory magic, because Leandro was protected against such magic by his wedding ring: a gold band with a roseate stone in the form of a heart, which was so securely welded to his finger that it could not be separated from it. Zulietta's failure to seduce him had only served to intensify her desire, which had turned into an indomitable passion.

Zulietta's seductive powers had more success with Bartolomeo Collatino, who became her instrument, charged with dispossessing Leandro of the protective ring by the only means possible—that of severing his finger. In the meantime, however, Maurizio Scamozzi had fallen madly in love with Zulietta and, enraged by her seduction of Barolomeo and intent on preventing her seduction of Leandro, he revealed the scheme to Caterina. Caterina, enraged in her turn, went to her father for help, but he, disapproving of her marriage, refused to assist her, and she turned instead to a youthful *bravo* nicknamed Tondino, who had rapidly built a reputation for recklessness, offering to appoint him as her cicisbeo if he could dispose of Bartolomeo surreptitiously.

At that point, the first Act came to an end, and there was an intermission—but no one moved from their seats. The sighted members of the audience seemed to me to be looking round suspiciously and anxiously, inspecting the masks around them, searching for clues as to the identity of the individuals behind the masks, but finding none.

Some of the characters featured in the original story had to be dead, I imagined, after all these years—but not, I now suspected, Zulietta or Caterina, who might or might not be the two women sitting in the boxes opposite. My companion had revealed himself, deliberately, to me but presumably not to anyone else, as Leandro, and had enabled me to see not merely his missing finger but the ring that had been stolen from it. Worn by whom? By a blind man or a sighted one? By a *bravo* who had stolen it or by someone who had merely purchased it as it passed from had to hand? At any rate, if appearances could be trusted, by someone young, who could not have featured in the original story.

All that passed through my mind in a flash, and would doubtless have provided food for thought during the entire entr'acte had not my companion's damaged hand fallen on my shoulder again, while his voice whispered in my ear:

"All this is trivial, my friend: mere human games, of no real consequence. You know who I really am, by name at least, but the version of my legend you have heard is greatly distorted."

The voice was strangely sonorous, and it had a curiously soothing effect on my confused mind; it drew my attention and focused it, causing everything else—not merely the theater and its bizarre audience but space and time themselves—to fade into the background. It was as if, for an immeasurable interval, nothing existed except that voice, and the story it was telling.

"You have heard legends of the war in heaven, and the expulsion of the fallen angels, and you have heard legends, too, of the expulsion of humans from the paradise in which they originally dwelt, but the drama your myth-makers have constructed from those events is only one of many representations that might be imagined. Let me offer you another.

"There was an age in which all God's creatures, angels and humans alike, dwelt in paradise, and that paradise was the earth, but the angels and the humans displeased their Creator, in various ways. Rebellious pride played a part—the egotism gifted to them with free will—and the principal manifestation of that pride was passion, which led to miscegenation between angels and humans, and some confusion between the kinds. For reasons known only to the Creator, that confusion offended him greatly, and he punished the offenders, angelic and human alike, by casting them out of paradise. He cast out all of the humans, but only a fraction of the angels, retaining those he considered to be innocent of offending him.

"The Creator did not do that by removing either the humans or the expelled angels to some other physical location, but by removing from them certain powers of perception. He expelled them simply by denying them the sight of paradise, and hence the mental experience—the perception of the beauty and the joy that were the essential aspects of paradise.

"He inflicted the additional punishment on humans of removing their ability to perceive and interact with the angels, thus putting an end to the possibility of further miscegenation, although it is arguable that the restriction penalized the angels too—all of them—by denying them the privilege of any longer being perceived by humans: a frustration that some of the angels felt more keenly than others, and the fallen angels that had loved human beings most keenly of all.

"To some extent, however, the damage already done could not be undone. The mingling of the species had introduced magical abilities of various kinds into certain members of the human race, which continued to surface occasionally, and somewhat unpredictably, as one generation followed another. The legacy of the original hybrids was progressively diluted, but never diminished in total. Most humans gifted with such abilities found it very difficult to control and exploit them, but some of those who attained a measure of control became aware of their hereditary aspects and attempted to seek out others of their kind and form families in which the gifts might be occasionally be reconcentrated.

"The fallen angels also retained a fugitive legacy from the days when they had been able to see and experience paradise, and the fact that they could still perceive humans, although humans could not perceive them, enabled them to act in certain cunning and limited ways to guide humans and influence their cultural evolution. That was, as you can probably imagine, a frustrating business, but they learned to be content with small successes, and their attempts to foster the residual magical powers that still existed, scattered here and there, among the human population, allowed them to hope that they would be able, from time to time, to assist at least some humans to perceive them, at least peripherally, uncertainly and temporarily.

"Some of the more ambitious fallen angels—the *philosophes* among them, as you might put it—even dared to dream that, by combining the residual powers of mercurial human magic with the ever-advancing capacities of reliable human technology, it might one day be possible to find a way to replace what the Creator had removed, and permit some individuals, human or angelic, to recover, if only partially and temporarily, the perception of paradise.

"Was that really possible? Who can tell? What form would that ingenious combination of magic and technology take? Would it be an optical instrument, like a lorgnette, a telescope or a microscope? Or might it be required to take a more drastic form: something that would not simply supplement the visual organ but replace it? The ambitious angels could not determine that in advance of the discovery—but they continued the exploratory quest, with the aid of human beings that they were capable of influencing and inspiring, one way or another. And some humans recruited to that cause inevitably became devout believers not only in the possibility of that success, but in the value of the prize that they sought.

"The miscegenation of the human and angelic races was more awkward and more perverse than the human imagination might readily assume, because the nature of angels is less stable that human myth-makers frequently assume. Angels are immortal, but their existence is intermittent rather than constant, and their forms—which might be more accurately described as their costumes, or their masks—are variable. They are not always perceptible, even to one another. As for the angelic qualities redistributed among the human species, they are similarly unstable and intermittent in their perceptible manifestations. Those circumstances further complicate the mission of those fallen angels determined to find a means of recovering the perception of paradise in a general, stable fashion that even the Creator could not take away again.

"Alas, I cannot yet provide you with a denouement to this story, because it has not yet reached its conclusion, and it is not yet possible to judge whether it will be possible to reach one in centuries or millennia to come, or ever. I and my kind, however, continue to hope and to strive, to do what we can, where and when we can, in the belief that no small step in the right direction, however trivial and likely to go awry, ought to be scorned. We make mistakes, because it is not merely human to err, and we have difficulty repairing them, because our capacity for working miracles is far more limited than myth-makers sometimes imagine. We also make progress, however, and have sometimes been able not only to allow humans to see us but also to interact with us in all kinds of ways, albeit sporadically.

"As a playmaker yourself, you will understand the awkwardness of that deficiency, from the viewpoint of a fellow playmaker like myself. You will understand my embarrassment in telling you a story without a neat ending, in building a fantasy without a resolution…but what choice do I have, given that the premises of the story do not permit any conclusion to be drawn, as yet? What choice do I have but to banish the narrative of my play to an entr'acte, something merely glimpsed, in the interstices of the world as it can presently be perceived, by the feeble eyes and minds that you and I possess, and the limited sight to which you and I are likewise condemned?"

The mutilated hand was raised from my shoulder then, as the curtain went up again and the second act of *Il Re giallo* began.

There had been a time lapse in the chronology of the drama, in which mysterious events had occurred. Bartolomeo Collatino had been found with his eyes excised, unable or unwilling to say exactly what had happened to him. Leandro de Mastropietro's finger had also been severed, and he too was either unable or unwilling to reveal the circumstances of its severing. Maurizio Scamozzi and Tondino disappeared, and no one knew whether to suspect Maurizio of having murdered Tondino and fled Venice or Tondino of having murdered Maurizio and fled. Zulietta and Caterina made wild accusations and issued dire threats against one another. Andrea Zellini and Peiro Beroviero made grim accusations and issued ominous threats against one another. Leandro, perhaps in the hope of restoring order and peace, or the desire to bring about a licensed vengeance, appealed to the King in Yellow for a Solomonic judgment.

The eponymous character finally appeared on stage, playing the role that theatrical jargon calls a *deus ex machina*, although, in the context of the present comedy, he was perhaps more closely akin to a *diabolus ex machina*. Sitting silently in judgment behind his yellow mask, he heard the various complaints and accusations, which were so inextricably confused that it was evident that no human power could possibly work out any viable compromise or treaty. And in the end, he came to a decision that none of the characters in the plot seemed to understand, let alone to accept.

The King in Yellow instructed Pietro Beroviero to give him two pairs of glass eyes, which Pietro—who, for some reason, appeared to be in the habit of carrying glass eyes about his person—immediately did. The King in Yellow then gripped two of the eyes in one hand and two in the other, and pronounced some kind of magical spell. He then informed the assembled characters that he had conferred on the pair of eyes held in his right hand the property of restoring to their wearer the ability, long lost by human beings as a result of the sin of Adam, to see paradise, while the pair in his left hand would restore to their wearer the ability to see angels.

The King in Yellow then gave the first pair of eyes to Caterina, and the second to Zulietta, and left the decision to them, with or without the guidance of their respective husbands, as to whether either of them would offer the pair they had to Bartoloeo Collatino, or whether they would dispose of them in some other fashion. He warned all the parties involved, however, that each pair would only work as a pair, and that if the four eyes were separated, or combined into pairs that did not match, they would be useless at best, and perhaps far worse than useless, in that the incomplete or confused sight they would grant a wearer or possessor would gradually drive him or her mad, condemning him or her to see and experience, not paradise, but a world from which all joy and beauty had been banished.

Having delivered that verdict, the King in Yellow then made as if to exit the stage—but he did not do so. Abruptly changing direction, instead of disappearing into the wings, he cleaved a path through the assembly of plaintiffs and came to the front of the stage to address the audience.

Thus far, everything in the play seemed to me to have been following a script slavishly, but now it seemed that the King in Yellow was improvising, for he lapsed from relatively formal Italian into Venetian dialect, and I suddenly found considerable difficulty in following what he was saying. The gist of it, however, was that the script of the play then required the characters, unable to accept his verdict as any kind of solution, to be begin contesting possession of the two pairs of eyes violently, and that the result of their conflict would be a disorderly brawl, in which the eyes would be separated. Caterina would retain one, and Zulietta another, but the other two would be carried away by others, whose identity the script did not reveal.

At that point, the actor said, the play as written had to end, in utter confusion—but he, personally, both as an actor and as a personification of the King in Yellow, found that conclusion direly unsatisfactory, just as he found the thirty-nine years of confusion and madness that had followed the actual events fictionalized in the play unsatisfactory. He therefore wanted to make a plea, that the various contending parties that had been gathered in the Teatro Festim on the eve of Lent, including the survivors of the original drama as well as all the individuals who had since become involved with the quest, should bring all four eyes together on to the stage, in order that someone devoid of eyes could identify the two that constituted the Portals of Paradise.

Then, he said, his desire was that, instead of inspiring madness, he could inspire sanity, and enable the various people ambitious to possess the eyes to settle their differences peacefully, and to collaborate in the restoration of the order that had been dramatically—whether tragically or comically—disrupted.

Then, silence fell.

No one shouted at the King in Yellow instructing him to take off his mask, thus giving him the opportunity to reply that he was not wearing one—which would have been absurd, because the play was, after all, merely a play, and the actor merely an actor, who was very obviously wearing a mask.

Even without that facilitating device, however, I was in no doubt that there was madness in the air, and that it only needed a spark to be ignited. Unlike a conventional *deus ex machina*, whose theatrical role was to sort out the confusion that the human characters were unable to sort out themselves, the King in Yellow, cast as he was a *diabolus ex machina*, was perhaps far more likely to sow and augment confusion than to soothe it, even while pleading for calm and order, and even if his plea was perfectly sincere.

Poor fellow, I thought. *He's trying to act in a godly manner, and doubtless doing his best, but what chance does he have with an audience like this one?*

The answer to that question, as you will have had no difficulty at all in guessing, was none.

XII

MADNESS

I took it for granted, of course, that the eyes that had been handed over to the actors on stage were mere props, simple pieces of glass with no supernatural properties whatsoever. The actors, however, must have got into the skin of their parts, because the actor playing Bartolomeo seemed very convincing as he hurled himself blindly upon the actress playing Zulietta and wrenched one of the eyes out of her hand—but he was instantly attacked himself by the actor playing Leandro. In the meantime, the actor playing Andrea Zellini hurled himself upon Caterina and wrenched one of the eyes from her grip, immediately prior to being attacked by the actor playing Pietro Beroviero.

After that, the scene on stage was nothing but a brawl.

What happened on the stage, however, was a mere figuration, still essentially fictional—and those actors who were armed were presumably only equipped with stage daggers incapable of inflicting mortal harm. What happened in the audience was a different matter.

I cannot describe the scene in minute detail, because of the limitation of my vision and my attention, but the main thread of the action was easy enough to follow, for a while. To begin with it seemed to me that at least a dozen and perhaps as many as twenty real blind men stood up in the audience, howling like wolves and bellowing like bulls as they urged their sighted companions to action. Those companions, I assumed, were mostly *bravi* of some kind, whether affiliated to the depleted guild or not, and most of them seemed to have been primed in advance with information as to who might be in possession of one or more glass eyes that were not mere stage props.

One of the Arlecchinos, possessed of a Stentorian voice, pointed a finger at one of the audience-members costumed as Capitan Spaventa. "That," he declared, "is the man who has two of the eyes."

The blind men could not see where he was pointing, but their sighted companions could—and the *bravos* could see, too, that the Spaventa in question seemed to be one of their own kind, or at least a man trained in fighting, for he was quick to draw his sword and move its point around him in an very purposeful fashion. Immediately, two other men, one costumed as Arlecchino and one as Brighella, closed ranks with him to his left and his right, with blades drawn.

"Very clever," Spaventa shouted, in English. "I see that a trap has been set, and that I have fallen into it. I admit, then, that the eyes that I have are not the ones you want. I cannot use them myself, but I have certainly tried their effect, as at least one Scaramucchia and two Arlec-chinos present here can attest—and every thief who had them before me has doubtless done likewise." He paused momentarily, and the voices of several blind men were, indeed, raised to testify that they had tried eyes shown to them by the Englishman, and found them useless.

"Everyone here knows that Zulietta Zellini still has one of the Por-tals of Paradise, unless it has been stolen from her" the Englishman shouted, while he and his auxiliaries continuing maneuvering their blades to keep their adversaries at bay—although had those adversar-ies acted in concert they could have overwhelmed the three by force of numbers in a trice. "Tondino, I think, at least believes that he has long had the other. If Zulietta and Tondino will make themselves known, we can hold the auction that was promised, and those who desire to do so can make their bids peacefully and honestly, as the King in Yellow has asked us all to do."

My companion's voice whispered in my ear: "He's wrong. The woman in the third box on the far side, who is not Zulietta, believes that she has three of the four eyes, and Tondino believes that he has two, albeit a mismatched pair—but there are at least two others here who firmly believe that they have each have one of the authentic eyes. Was there ever a legend that did not give rise to fakes and forgeries in profusion?"

Capitan Spaventa was still looking around wildly and the hedge of menacing blades—but they did not strike at him; the violence was still in suspension. "Tondino must be here!" the Englishman shouted. "Come on, Tondino, the time has come to show yourself." He was still speaking in his native tongue, but at least half the embers of the audi-ence could understand what he was saying well enough, and even those who did not must have understood his challenge to Tondino.

But Tondino did not show himself.

Instead, the woman in the beaded dress, in the box nearest the stage on the far side of the theater, stood up, and all attention immediately swiveled in her direction. "Your arithmetic is at fault, brigand," she said, "just as the eyes you have are mere glass, for I swear that this one has never left my possession since my father first handed it to me. I'll give ten thousand lira to any man who can provide me with its pair, or take ten for anyone who wants to buy it from me."

And the masked woman held up a glass eye.

"She's lying, and desperately." my companion whispered. "She's some adventuress, perhaps put up to the imposture by Tondino, but quite possibly a victim of her own madness."

For few seconds, no one moved—but then a white-clad Pierrot whose face was completely masked and whose conical cap seemed to weigh too heavily upon his head, said in Italian: "The Englishman has been deceived. I am not Tondino, but I do have one of the authentic eyes, which I am ready and willing to submit to auction, if the King in Yellow will agree to serve as auctioneer, along with the one offered by the lady clad in beads."

"You would be bidding for trash!" a new voice cried—that of the woman in the third box from the stage. "How many more false eyes are here? If there is to be any settlement here, however contrived, we must first determine the two authentic pairs."

Immediately several of the blind men, including the Arlecchino and the Scaramucchias that had earlier endorsed the Englishman's claim, began shouting that they could do that, and volunteering their services.

The King in Yellow was still standing at the front of the stage, with the comedic brawl in full swing behind him. He held up his arms, but silence did not fall in response, either behind him or in front, and he to had to shout to make himself heard.

"My friends!" he cried. "We must settle, first, how many eyes are here. Until we know that, we cannot even begin to distinguish the authentic pairs.

His was, I suppose, the fragile voice of sanity, and had it been heeded, all the members of the audience who thought themselves to be in possession of one of the four magical eyes might conceivably have come forward, the eyes might have been collected, whether there were eight or twelve or twenty, and the men devoid of eyes could have begun testing them, two by two—but who, even in that unlikely case, would have been prepared to trust the testimony of the testers? And even if that step in the process could have been completed, would that unruly crowd have settled down to an orderly auction, at the conclusion of which everyone would have accepted the result?

No, obviously not. Madness had to prevail, eventually if not instantly—but how destructive would it be?

Perhaps some of those present believed that they knew which of their fellows had custody of one or more of the original eyes—I will not say authentic, because I could not see an atom of solid evidence within the welter of fantasies to suggest that any of them had real magical properties—but the likelihood is that most of those who had none at all were simply avid to possess as many as they could accumulate.

The English Spaventa and his two henchmen were the most obvious target of attack, and they were attached. So was the Pierrot who had unwisely declared himself. So was the fake Caterina di Mastropietro, although her companion, fighting from the edge of the box against two would-be thieves, had such a considerable positional advantage that his attackers had no evident chance of swift success.

I turned to look at my companion.

"You contrived this!" I said, accusingly.

"Did I?" he countered. "I took a hand, to be sure, once I discovered—belatedly, I fear—what was going on, but you know perfectly well who first set out to contrive it: the lady who summoned you to join her cast of players, and deliver her message to another of her dupes, aided and abetted by the English trickster."

"Is that lady Zulietta Zellini?" I queried.

"Of course not," he replied. "My darling Caterina killed Zulietta Zellini many years ago, shortly after killing her swine of a husband. She was a real she-devil in those days. That's why she had to leave Venice; there was no hiding place even in Murano at that time for someone who had a price put on her head by the Mastropietros and the Zellinis."

"The lady is Caterina, then?" I asked, although the answer followed logically.

"Of course. She really does have one of the original eyes, but as for the other two in her possession, I doubt their authenticity…nor would I care to guarantee either of those Tondino has. Perhaps we shall see—but first things first."

And with that, he leapt over the edge of the box and down to the floor below, leaving me alone. I stood up and leaned over, to watch his progress across the floor.

At that point, I swear, although I acknowledge that it makes no sense in terms of the chronology of what followed, I heard the clocks of Giudetta chime, and immediately jumped to the conclusion that it was the first of the twelve chimes of midnight, rung by all the bells in Venice to signal that Lent would begin in eleven seconds' time.

Was I simply mistaken? Perhaps—but if so, what was the chime? Perhaps a mere auditory illusion—but it seemed to me that time simply went awry, and that its flow *congealed*.

Nothing stopped, but everything—or *almost* everything—seemed to slow down momentarily. It seemed to me that I had been gripped by a tremendous force, which made the least action improbably difficult. A reflex had been raising my hand to my mouth, but my arm seemed all of a sudden to be moving through treacle rather than air. My thoughts, on the other hand, raced ahead without the least impedance…and my thoughts were not the only free agency.

A second chime, real or illusory, sounded while my actions were frozen, seemingly extended infinitely, although I might simply have lost track of its duration, but I have no memory of hearing any more for a considerable interval thereafter.

As soon as the congelation of time relaxed and I was capable of normal action again, the door of the box opened behind me, and I turned round abruptly, to find myself facing the King in Yellow—not the actor on the stage, who was still standing there, wand in hand, helplessly sandwiched between the contrived chaos on the stage behind him and the authentic chaos in the auditorium, but the one from the box next door.

He had already opened his wand to reveal the blade, and he was already raising it in order to direct it at me in an admittedly desultory fashion, more as a precautionary defense than an attack. I had dropped my own wand, however, and I drew my rapier instead, instantly, and with complete confidence in my ability to hold him off by means of the longer blade. Before he could change his stance in order to pose a threat against me, I had the tip of my own blade at his throat, and I forced him back against the wall.

"That's hardly fair, Leandro," he said, mildly. "I came prepared for an honorable settlement of our differences, if necessary, with equal weapons, but I'd far rather follow the other King's advice and talk peace, if you're willing."

"Perhaps that would be agreeable," I replied, in Italian, "if I were actually Leandro."

For a moment, I had the impression that the eyes behind the yellow mask were startled, but he simply let his own blade dangle, shook his head, and said: "The angelic Englishman. I should have guessed. Did he actually plant you in Paris, as bait, or did he merely take advantage of Caterina's delusion?"

"In view of the fact that my weapon is at your throat, I rather think that I have the right to ask the questions," I told him.

"Fine," he said, shrugging his shoulders. "Go ahead."

"First, who are you?"

"Giovanni Beroviero," he said.

"Son of Pietro?"

"No, grandson."

"Caterina's nephew?"

"Yes."

"And who was the man to whom I delivered her message—the one calling himself Mercutio?"

"That's Tondino, of course—didn't Leandro tell you?"

"Tondino! How did he lose his eyes?"

"They were put out by Maurizio Scamozzi, in swift reprisal for what he did to Barolomeo. That's why Pietro made two pairs of eyes. The *bravi* were still violent in those days, at least with one another. Tondino got his revenge, though. somehow. Maurizio was dead within a year."

"Does Tondino really have one of the supposedly-magical eyes that your grandfather made?"

"Caterina certainly thinks so—but she also thinks that the three she has are genuine and that you're an angel, so the probability is that she's quite mad. Even so, family is family...and I really thought that I might at least be able to talk some sanity into Leandro, if I offered to return his ring. Apparently not. The fact that he put you in his costume testifies to a certain diabolical intelligence in his planning, though. Perhaps Caterina's right about him."

"Right?" I queried.

"She thinks he's an angel too—albeit a fallen one. She thinks the three eyes she has include the lesser pair, which is why she's convinced that one of the ones Tondino has is the companion to her third."

"And who's the Capitan Spaventa who dropped out of the game when he realized that it was too rich?"

"Oh, he's just an English adventurer who picked up the legend while guiding groups of Tourists and thought he could exploit it, and Caterina too, with the aid of fakes of his own. Perhaps you know him—he calls himself Lord Kenavan, although God alone knows what his real name is?"

"And the Pierrot who offered an eye to partner the one possessed by the woman posing as your aunt?"

"Don't know him. Some other deluded idiot. Far from the only one, I'd guess. My aunt and the Englishman have certainly staged this farce effectively, although it seems to be going horribly awry."

"And where did you get Leandro's ring?" I asked, finally.

"From the person who cut his finger off, of course. She's had it for thirty-nine years."

"Caterina?"

"Yes. In fact, speaking of my dear aunt, the family won't forgive me if I allow her to be murdered, and since Leandro has left you here to put me off the track…" He looked down at the floor. "Which one is he? Oh, I have it—he's the fellow in a black hood dressed as you've been dressed these last three days. Damn! Have you actually made a pact with him to hold me off while he does what he came here to do?"

"Murder Caterina?"

"Perhaps. I fear so. Either way, I'd like to catch him if I can, and try to make sure that this farce doesn't get any further out of hand than it already has. May I?"

I lowered my sword. "Go on, then," I said.

Immediately, he leapt over the edge of the box exactly as Leandro had, with far more natural entitlement to the agility of his leap.

I believed him. He was, after all the first person I'd encountered who had actually given me straight answers to the questions that were seething in my mind. Were they true? Looking back now, I'm by no means sure that they were—but at the time, while the chimes of midnight were still strangely suspended, I believed him. I believed that Mercutio was Tondino, that Caterina was completely mad, and that she really did think that I was an angel and that Leandro was the Devil…or a fallen angel, at least. Given what my companion had whispered in my ear during the entr'acte, I had to suppose that Leandro believed it too, or was at least prepared to entertain the fantasy.

Could I be sure, though, that it was all delusion? Could I be absolutely certain that Leandro was not, in fact, a fallen angel?

I turned my attention back to the auditorium, but it seemed strangely distant and detached. I think that I heard the clocks of Venice chime again—or at least the clocks of Guidecca—but I had no idea what they were chiming. If the ones I heard before really had been chiming twelve, the other ten should have finished long ago…unless time actually had gone mad in the wake of *Il Re giallo*.

At any rate, it seemed to me the wings of time began to beat a little more rapidly once my counterpart King in Yellow had leapt out of the box. Perhaps the wings in question were also beating a little more forcefully than before, in order to make up a little of their apparent loss, but it might simply have been that events were moving with astonishing rapidity.

What was happening on the floor below was utter chaos. Sighted men were falling upon blind men in order to wrench away their masks, seemingly convinced that one or more of them might be hiding the eyes that Pietro Beroviero had made, for his daughter or the Devil, perhaps to serve as stakes in a contest between the experienced bravo Bartolomeo Collatino and the ambitious newcomer Tondino, to determine which of them would win the affection of Zulietta Zellini…or perhaps for some other motive entirely.

Two Pierrots had already been knocked down, although neither white costume was strained with blood, so I presumed that they had not actually been stabbed. A third was holding a dagger high above his head, but that was not bloodstained either; I could not tell which of the three was the one who had unwisely declared that he had one of the eyes in his possession. Two Captain Spaventas were fighting a fierce duel, with their great cloaks flapping like the wings of giant eagles. Brighellas were brawling, and Pantalones were punching one another. There seemed to be Arlecchinos everywhere.

It only took me a moment or two to spot my erstwhile companion from the box, wielding a naked sword and carving theatrically this way and that as he tried to make his way through the confusion on the floor, but his blade did not seem to be making any lethal contact, even though people kept lurching into his path. He kept shoving them aside, but was still having difficulty completing his trajectory toward the third box on the far side, where his wife Caterina was sitting, resting her gloved hands lightly on the cushioned rail, perhaps watching with interest and waiting patiently for some kind of outcome, although it seemed more likely to me that she was numb with shock, watching her crazy plans fall apart and her insensate hopes for the future evaporate.

The King in Yellow who had the supposedly magical ring set off across the floor in the wake of the hooded man while I watched, the blade withdrawn from his wand still naked, but the other brawlers kept getting in his way too, and he was having equal difficulty maintaining his equilibrium and his progress.

The door of my box opened yet again, and an Arlecchino slipped in, followed by a blind man, whom inspired guesswork allowed me to recognize in spite of his black mask.

"He's in here," said Arlecchino, gazing disdainfully at my rapier, which I tried half-heartedly to raise, although he had not made any aggressive gesture toward me.

"Giovanni," said Tondino, tiredly, "can we not settle this matter between the two of us? I came here in good faith, trusting in your guarantee of safe conduct."

"If I were Giovanni," I said, tiredly, "he would surely say yes, but I'm not."

Arlecchino groaned. "It's the blond Englishman," he said. "He was in on it all along."

A denial would have been futile.

"Give me his hand," said Tondino, immediately.

I surrendered my right hand meekly enough. Cheiromancer or not, the pseudonymous Mercutio was evidently able to recognize instantly that my hand was not Giovanni Beroviero's or Leandro di Mastropietro's.

"Damnation!" he said. "Where's the other one gone?"

"Fighting his way across the floor," said Arlecchino. "Please don't ask me to chase him." He turned his attention back to me, and switched to English: "That yellow devil's not Leandro, I presume?"

"No," I agreed. "That one really is Giovanni."

"He's irrelevant—just kill him, and let's go," said Tondino, petulantly—but Arlecchino made no move to obey, even though he still did not seem impressed by my rapier.

"I'm not killing anyone," he retorted, bluntly, in Italian, "and I'm staying here, at least for now. I told you this was a fool's errand at the very beginning."

"Can you see Caterina?" Tondino demanded.

"Oh yes—she's sitting in her box, with her latest cicisbeo, either as cool as ice or paralyzed with shock. Who can tell? There's some fellow clad in black who seems to be trying to reach her, though. That might be Leandro." Again, he turned to me, but not to ask for confirmation of his identification of Leandro. Switching back to English, he asked, bluntly: "Are you with Kenavan?"

"No," I said.

"Caterina? Leandro?"

"No. They just tricked me into delivering messages for them."

"Then why are you here? And how did you get in?"

"I was invited," I told him, with a slight laugh. "By the Devil or Leandro—I'm still not sure which. He gave me this pass." I showed him the page in my notebook. "You don't, by any chance, know what language it's written in?"

"It's not a language," Arlecchino replied, sounding even wearier than Tondino. "It's the secret code of the guild of *bravi*. Leandro isn't supposed to know it, but I doubt that there are any secrets left nowadays. What a mess this is!"

"At least Signor Tondino has some reason for hoping that the eye that's a counterpart to his own might be of use to him," I observed. "How many others drawn here by Caterina and Kenevan can say even that much?"

"Sheer madness," Arlecchino agreed, with a sigh. "Why did you dress up as Giovanni?"

"I didn't," I told him. "Leandro sent me the costume. I had no idea that it would duplicate anyone's."

The bravo nodded. "Sheer madness," he said, again.

"I'm not paying you for your scornful opinions, damn it!" Tondino snapped. "I'm paying you to help me get my hands on Caterina's eyes. "Since Giovanni's not here, I suggest you go after him, or go direct to Caterina."

Arlecchino rolled his eyes. "If you could see what I can see, my dear cheiromancer," he said, "you'd understand my refusal. You're not paying me to kill anyone, let alone risk getting killed myself. When everything calms down, I'll do what I can, if there's anything left to do. Until then, we're both better off out of harm's way."

He looked significantly at the rapier, and I replaced it in its sheath, to confirm that he and his master really were out of harm's way while they remained in the box. I also put my yellow hood down, donned the black cloak that I had worn while coming to the theater, and took off my mask. Although I hadn't heard the twelfth stroke of midnight, I felt morally certain that Lent really must have begun by now.

Arlecchino nodded in acknowledgement, but didn't unmask himself.

And together, we watched the conflict reach its end.

XIII

THE RETURN OF SANITY

On the stage, the actors, all of whom had ceased the mock-fighting that their script required of them, had gathered at the edge of the stage to watch the riot on the floor. The actor plating the King in Yellow had pushed back his hood, as I had, and taken off his mask, to reveal a perfectly ordinary face, whose expression was more disappointed than bewildered. Evidently, he had not expected his plea—which I now supposed had been just as carefully scripted as the rest of the play—to succeed. He too had expected the madness to explode.

Except that, although the madness had definitely exploded, it was all somewhat half-hearted. I was reminded of my impression of the Carnival on Friday and Saturday, as a tired performance going through the motions. Yes, there were blades being waved in profusion, and punches being thrown, but most of the screaming and fulminating was coming from the blind men, urging on their sighted hirelings and helpers. Very few, if any of those hirelings and helpers had the motivation or the stomach for an all-out fight. Like Tondino's Arlecchino, in spite of some of them being members of the secret guild of *bravi*, or perhaps because of it, they had no appetite for murder in a cause so ludicrous, let alone for putting their own lives at risk. They were making a great deal of noise, but almost without exception, they seemed perfectly content to make noise.

The two Pierrots that I had seen knocked down hauled themselves up to a sitting in position, nursing their bruises, and the pools of blood on the floor were small in size and few and far between. The Capitan Spaventa that had been identified to me as Lord Kanevan had already disappeared from the auditorium, taking his auxiliaries with him. I suspected that no one had even bothered to dispossess them of their glass eyes, given that those two were known for certain to be fakes. How many other eyes Caterina's agents, or the agents of other interested parties, had managed to collect from the less wary individuals attracted by the possibility of an auction, I could not tell, but I was certain that the collection would be futile.

The madness in the hall had not proved as infectious as it might have done, and as the crowd thinned out, more rapidly by the minute, the insanity that remained was concentrated in the imprecations of a few impotent blind men and, arguably, the one sighted man who still seemed to consider that he had a mission to fulfill: Leandro di Mastropietro.

I say arguably because, by now, I was no more convinced that Leandro was mad than I was convinced that he was the Devil. I had begun to suspect, that he, too, was more intent on putting on a show than actually murdering Caterina, even if that was his intention if he contrived to reach her. I didn't know anything about the layout of the theater, so I didn't know whether there would have been any easier route from our box to hers than the one he had taken through the turbulent crowd, nor was I entirely convinced that he had not known for certain which of the two women in the boxes opposite was his estranged wife until the other had made her false claim.

Whatever the truth of the matter, though, it seemed to me that his charge across the floor was more comedy than earnest drama, and that the mighty leap from the back of a sofa that enabled him to grip the edge of the box and swing himself over acrobatically, while Caterina, getting up precipitately from her chair and stepping back in apparent panic, hampered her own defender, was pure theater.

Once Leandro had reached the box, however, Caterina's companion was able to get between the man and his wife, and engage the former in combat with a flourish befitting a Capitan Spaventa. That, at least, seemed honest, as steel clashed and hands grappled, and I thought for a moment that one of the two was bound to be badly cut. With another acrobatic twist, however, Leandro swung his opponent back against the rail of the box, and with a swift heave of which one would not have thought a man in is sixties capable, threw Il Capitano over it, to fall heavily on the floor below.

Then, as Caterina tried to escape through the door, which she had not been able to open previously for lack of room, Leandro slammed it shut in front of her, trapping her, and then pressed her against it, with the point of his sword at her throat.

He could have killed her then, with a single thrust, but he only snatched her purse, and tipped its contents out on to the floor of the box.

Then, methodically, he brought his boot-heel down, heavily, three times.

I could not see what effect the blows had with my own eyes, but it was easy enough to guess what he must be stamping on, and what the effect of his stamping must have been.

Caterina screamed: a terrible scream of anguish that instantly put a stop to the few remaining scuffles that were still going on.

Then Leandro reached into his own pocket and brought out a fourth glass eye, which he held up, so that it caught the light, and so that everyone still present in the room could see it. Then he dropped that one too, and smashed his heel down upon it.

So much, I thought, *for the quest for the Portals of Paradise.*

The legend might survive, I knew. There had been other glass eyes in the room apart from Kenavan's fakes—perhaps as many as six or eight—but the four that had been broken had been those held by Caterina di Mastropietro and her husband, two of the people present when the original distribution had been made. It would require a frank defiance of the esthetics of legend to believe that the smashing of those four had not, at the very least, destroyed one of each magical pair.

"What happened?" Tondino demanded, after Caterina's scream had died away, with an edge of panic in his voice.

Arlecchino did not want to answer him, so I stepped into the breach. "It's over, Signor," I said. "Leandro has smashed all of Caterina's glass baubles and one other. Even if one of the eyes you have is genuine, it no longer has a counterpart. The Portals of Paradise are gone, and so is the gift of seeing angels, at least until some talented descendant of Pietro Beroviero can forge more, with or without the aid of the Devil, or the King in Yellow. For the time being, the madness has been stamped out."

The eyeless man's groan was hollow and heart-rending, but there was a hint of inevitability about it—a final acceptance of the hopelessness of his quest: a hopelessness that he must always have suspected, and had only kept at bay for so long by the effort of obsession.

Giovanni Beroviero, who was a much younger man, contrived to match Leandro's leap, and hauled himself into the box.

Silence had fallen in the hall now, even among the blind, and Giovanni's voice was clearly audible, saying: "For the love of God, Leandro, leave her alone. She's only a poor old woman; her sins are thirty-nine years old and she can't do any more harm to anyone. Hasn't she suffered enough?" The dagger he had unsheathed from his wand was still in his hand, but he did not make any conspicuous show of threatening Leandro with it. For the moment, at least, he was relying on his powers of gentle persuasion.

I think that Leandro could have killed both of them, if he had really been determined to do so—but he was not.

Leandro let the point of the sword fall, describing a long vertical line in front of his wife, but without touching her costume, let alone her flesh. When the threat of the blade was removed, she collapsed to her knees, sobbing.

Leandro turned to Giovanni them, and put out his left hand, palm up.

"Give me the ring," he said.

"Gladly," said Giovanni Beroviero. "I brought it for no other purpose. He detached it from his finger and handed it over. In the absence of a ring finger, Leandro slipped it on to the little finger of his left hand, clenched the fist, and held it in front of Caterina's lowered eyes.

"Bound forever," he said. "*Forever*. I know what that means, although you never did, harlot."

Then he pushed her aside, opened the door of the box, stepped through it, and disappeared.

I looked at Arlecchino. "Well, Signor Playmaker," he said, in English, "how do you like the new Venetian comedy?"

"Very striking," I murmured, "But I'm in two minds about the improvisation."

"Thirty years ago, in my father's day," he said, "it would not have ended so tamely, but Venice is not what she was. She's close to exhaustion, and I fear for her future."

I put my hand on Tondino's shoulder. "I'm sorry, my friend," I said. "I can't believe that the eyes would have done what was claimed, but I am truly sorry that you didn't get a chance to try them." I thought that was generous of me, after he had told Arlecchino to kill me, albeit in a fit of pique.

The blind man reached up and took the hand I had placed on his shoulder. He ran the fingers of his other hand over it, but only lightly. He had read it before. "A long life," he said, bitterly, "and prosperous. You have no idea how I envy you, Signor Gabriel—but even so, I wish you well. I'm not what I was either, and closer to exhaustion than the city."

When I arrived in the open air outside the theater, I took a deep breath. Then I began to look around, for Leandro di Mastropietro's black hood and costume, or for the cloak of a Capitan Spaventa which might perhaps contain Lord Kenavan. There was no one.

I wondered, briefly, whether I ought to wait for Caterina to emerge, on Giiovanni's arm and surrounded by her bravi—but what would have been the point? What could I possibly have found to say to her?

I walked back to the water's edge, where boatmen were already clustered, evidently having been alerted to the impending exodus from the Teatro Festim some time before. One of them took me back to Santa Croce, from whose shore I only had a short walk back to the hotel.

I reached it at about two o'clock in the morning. Uncle Jerome had not returned, but I no longer had the mental energy to worry about him. I shrugged of the concealing cloak, stripped off my King in Yellow costume and went to bed.

XIV

UNCLE JEROME'S RETURN

When I woke up the next morning, Uncle Jerome was sitting in an armchair beside my bed, waiting for me to open my eyes. Once I had rubbed the sleep away, and had sat up, he said: "I'm sorry I missed your play. Would you believe that that swine Kenavan drugged my wine?"

"Actually," I said, "I certainly would believe it. All of this is his fault."

"That's a coincidence," said Uncle Jerome. "According to him, it's all yours."

"I'll be happy to debate the point with him."

"You won't have the chance. He's gone. He said that he would have had to leave anyway, even if the plan had worked, but that he'd hoped that he wouldn't have to leave empty-handed, and not because he'd crossed swords with half a dozen members of the guild of *bravi*. He said that he barely escaped with his life."

"He's exaggerating," I said.

"About the half-dozen *bravi?*"

"No, but about barely escaping with his life. If they'd actually wanted to kill him, they would have done so. They were just driving him away. And if he had been hurt, it certainly wouldn't have been my fault. Did he tell you what he was trying to do.?"

"Convince some mad old lady to buy some glass beads from him."

"Why on earth did he think he'd be able to get away with it?"

"She was already an established mark, apparently. She first went to Paris with a Venetian adventurer named Giacomo Casanova, who posed as a magician, and in the course of their affair he got the whole story out of her that you told me two days ago. When his imposture ran out she fell into the clutches of another trickster named Balsamo, who called himself Count Cagliostro. By the time he'd finished with her, he had her fully convinced that he'd given her the ability to detect angels in our midst, fallen and otherwise. Kenavan knew all about the legend of the Portals from previous visits to Venice in the course of his excursions as a bear-leader, and he knew all about Caterina too.

"When he noticed that the lady had taken a fancy to you, he set out to out-Casanova Casanova and out-Cagliostro Cagliostro, and he persuaded her to head for Venice at top speed, wait for you to arrive there and then make use of you as the messenger you were supposed to be, albeit unknown to yourself. How much he contributed to the plan to lure the other custodians of the eyes into a confrontation, I don't know, but neither of them expected so many worms to crawl out of the wood-work—the world is more rotten than we sometimes suspect, my lad.

"Apparently, you threw a spanner in the works during that very first meeting, when you told her you already knew about the performance at the Festim, even though you'd only arrived in Venice that day, and let her know that Leandro was in town, masquerading as the Devil. He had a great deal of difficulty after that, persuading her that everything might still go smoothly—perhaps unwisely, as they clearly didn't. She was also distraught, apparently, because she had been intent on seducing you during the rendezvous in Murano, but when the time came, she didn't even dare to try. She'd lost confidence in her abilities as a temptress, and couldn't bear to take the risk of exposing herself to possible scorn or laughter when you discovered her true age.

"Anyway, when I let slip to Kenavan yesterday that not only were you intending to go to the Festim but that I had insisted on going with you, he evidently decided that I was one complication too many, and put me to sleep almost round the clock, in his hotel room. I was still there, and very groggy, when he got back from the Festim himself, having failed to auction his worthless baubles and, according to him, having had to fight his way out against overwhelming odds.

"He nearly had to fight his way out again when he told me about the riot, but he assured me that you were safe in a box and well out of harm's way. I told him before he went, though, that if any harm came to you, I'd come after him, and that he certainly wouldn't get away un-scathed a second time."

"The man's a fool." I said.

"Agreed. I asked him why he didn't just try to sell the baubles to her in Paris, but he said that she already knew who he was, and that he absolutely had to work the deception wearing a mask—for which the Carnival provided the ideal opportunity, not only for him to maintain his incognito but also to hide amid a bunch of bauble-hawkers. As you say, a perfect fool. But it really wasn't you who messed his project up, was it?"

"No," I said. "It was the Devil—or Leandro de Mastropietro, or perhaps both, on account of their being one and the same, or at last pretending to be."

"Caterina's husband? He's still alive?"

"Apparently. Theirs was a love match you see—they were both young, hardly out of their twenties when the affair blew up. I'm still not sure how many adulteries there were, or exactly who slept with whom and when, but there were more than enough to stir up some ugly passions, and then to prompt the fantasy of the Portals of Paradise…if it was a fantasy."

"You can't think otherwise."

"No," I admitted, a trifle regretfully, "I can't. But Leandro spun me a fine story offering an alternative interpretation of what had happened, and I can't help thinking that it deserved to be more than mere froth. Fallen angel or not, he's a first-rate storyteller, albeit a little too flamboyant for my taste."

"Tell me," he demanded.

I gave him a succinct account of the story that my companion in the box at the Festim had told me during the entr'acte.

"Very ingenious," said Uncle Jerome. "You ought to put it in a play some day."

"Perhaps I will," I said.

"By the way," he said, "While you were still asleep, I sent the Misses Harrington an invitation to tea this afternoon. I should have done it yesterday, obviously, but I was otherwise occupied, as you know. I hope they won't take offense at the delay, and put it down to simple discretion. With any luck, we'll have a reply by noon, and then we'll know, one way or the other."

"They'll accept." I said.

"Are you that certain of the impression you made?"

"I have the face of an angel," I told him. "Once the initial barrier came down…and in any case, I have the Devil's word for it. Other miracles are mostly beyond his scope, it seems, but amorous passion is within his purview. He's not really in my debt any more, since he got me into the Festim, but he did that partly for his own purposes, so a small extra gesture to square the account is still in order."

"If you'll take my advice," said Unle Jerome, "you'll never joke like that with Miss Adelaide, and certainly not with the maiden aunt."

"I won't," I promised.

And, as you know full well, since Adelaide and I were married for thirty-nine years, I never did. In fact, I never told this story to anyone except Uncle Jerome, just in case a whisper of it got back to her. I honestly don't know how she'd have reacted if I told her that there was a possibility, however slim, that ours was a match made by the Devil rather than forged in Heaven, but I never dared take the risk. It can't hurt her now, God rest her soul.

I won't say that the marriage was perfect, because, as Mercutio the Cheiromancer told me, the course of amour never does run completely smooth, but I always took his advice, and obtained full value from its paradisal aspects, and never lost sight of my good fortune in having that tiny fraction of paradise in which to dwell, intermittently.

I haven't seen the Devil since, and if he really was only mere and mortal Leandro de Mastropietro, he must be long dead by now—but if that was merely a costume he put on for a while, who can tell when or where I might bump into him again? I rather hope that I do, because I have even more questions to ask him now than the ones I could imagine then, and not all of them are to do with stagecraft and the theory of comedy.

I've never been able to believe a word that he told me, of course, but a skeptic has the duty to doubt everything, including us own unbelief, and man who prides himself on being a *philosophe* and a playmaker—albeit, I fear, a rather unsuccessful one—has to be prepared to keep an open mind. That explains why, wherever I've been during the last forty years, I've always carried a hip-flask full of water drawn from a pure spring.

I don't suppose I'll ever need it, but where's the harm?

If, by chance, I ever do meet the Devil again, he's sure to have a thirst—and whatever people may say about him, I know for sure that he does appreciate acts of kindness, and I really can't believe that he actually wants the favors he does in return to generate as much mayhem and madness as the ring he gave to Pietro Beroviero and the glass eyes that he charmed for him.

www.ingramcontent.com/pod-product-compliance
Lightning Source LLC
Chambersburg PA
CBHW050757250626
47155CB00005B/2104